"I must go, Rebecca,"
Piers said. "I must."

Rebecca propped herself up on one elbow, unknowingly provocative. "Are you running away, Piers?" she asked softly.

"Yes! Yes, I am," he said, his eyes surveying her with devastating intensity. "I find I cannot destroy such innocence!"

Rebecca's frown deepened. "Piers, I haven't asked you for anything—I don't expect anything. I know what I'm doing."

"I doubt it, Rebecca," he muttered grimly. "Please don't make it any harder for me than it is. For the first time in my life I have found something beautiful, something worthwhile—and God help me, I cannot take it!" Rebecca stared unbelievingly as he went swiftly out the door....

Other titles by

ANNE MATHER
IN HARLEQUIN PRESENTS

ANNE MATHER

a distant sound of thunder

Harlequin Books

TORONTO • LONDON • NEW YORK • AMSTERDAM
SYDNEY • HAMBURG • PARIS

Harlequin Presents edition published September 1973
ISBN 0-373-70520-4

Second printing November 1973
Third printing July 1974
Fourth printing August 1974
Fifth printing May 1976
Sixth printing September 1976
Seventh printing February 1977
Eighth printing March 1977
Ninth printing December 1978

Original hardcover edition published in 1972
by Mills & Boon Limited

PART ONE

CHAPTER ONE

THE velvet dusk of evening was spreading its cloak over the island, stilling the chattering minah birds and dimming the brilliance of the exotic frangipani and flame trees. A welcome, cooling breeze sprang up as the sun sank below the tangled web of the jungle behind the villa, pushing probing fingers against Rebecca's hot forehead as she emerged from her patient's room and closed the door thankfully. The humidity throughout the long day had been exhausting and not even the air-conditioning could cope entirely with the damp heat. Rebecca ran a weary hand through the thick silky fairness of the curls on her brow and longed for the luxury of the shower she would soon be taking. Adele had been particularly trying today, but she was asleep now and for a few hours her time was her own.

As she passed along the terrazzo tiling of the hall she glanced automatically towards the wide windows which in daylight gave a magnificent view of the lush green grass which was all that separated the villa from the palm-fringed reaches of the beach. Beyond the stretch of silvery coral sand surged the brilliant waters of the Pacific and Rebecca never tired of marvelling at the natural beauty of her surroundings. It was worth the humidity, the persistent hum of insects, the sometimes nauseating aroma of drying copra, and even Adele's often cruel contentiousness.

Now she made her way to her room and stripping off her uniform and underclothing she went into the adjoining bathroom. The chill of the water took her breath away as she twisted and turned beneath the shower and she gasped pleasurably. She was vigorously towelling herself dry when the doorbell chimed.

At once she stopped what she was doing and frowned. What an annoying thing to have happened! It was the servants' night off and she was alone in the villa, apart from the sleeping Adele, of course, and she would not remain sleeping long if whoever it was who was calling persisted in ringing the bell. She sighed exasperatedly. Perhaps they would see no lights and go away. She hoped so. She couldn't imagine who it might be. Adele had few friends and it was not a night that the doctor usually called.

The bell rang again, and Rebecca pressed her lips together in annoyance. She would have to answer the door. There was nothing else for it. Thrusting the towel aside, she reached for her housecoat, a silky garment in rather an attractive shade of apricot. Her hair was a tangled mass of curls, and she had no time to comb it now. Smoothing it with a careless hand, she left the bathroom and walked impatiently along the corridor to the front door. In daylight a mesh screen was all that covered the entrance, but tonight the doors were closed and secured and she was loath to open them to admit ... who?

She slid back the bolt, turned the key and opened the door a few inches. In the faint light emanating from the hall she could see a tall man waiting outside and for a moment her heart flipped a beat.

'Yes?' she murmured tentatively, but to her surprise the man stepped forward, gently but firmly propelling the door back so that he could step into the hall. 'Just a moment——' began Rebecca indignantly, and the man inclined his head with frowning speculation.

'Your pardon, *mademoiselle*,' he exclaimed, his accent unmistakably French. 'For the moment I mistook you for Adele's maidservant. My apologies for startling you.'

Rebecca was trying to control the hot flush that was

6

running up her body and engulfing her at the realisation that she was wearing only the clinging apricot gown and this man was standing, regarding her indolently with dark eyes which were nevertheless intense. He was one of the most attractive men Rebecca had ever seen, but this knowledge only added to her confusion.

'Miss—Miss St. Cloud has retired for the night,' she informed him uncomfortably. 'I—I am her nurse.'

The man glanced round the wide hall with inscrutable eyes and then returned his gaze to Rebecca. 'Ah, so. I should have realised perhaps, but my plane was delayed...' He lifted his shoulders in a careless gesture. 'No matter, I will not disturb her now. Will you tell her in the morning that I called?'

Rebecca swallowed hard. 'Who—who shall I say has called, *monsieur*?'

The man raised his dark eyebrows for a moment, and then shrugged. 'Just tell her it was St. Clair, *mademoiselle*. She will know who that is.' He studied her flushed cheeks with faint amusement. 'And you, *mademoiselle*? Do you have a name?'

'Er—Lindsay—Nurse Lindsay,' replied Rebecca jerkily.

He regarded her intently for a moment. 'Nurse Lindsay,' he repeated slowly. 'You have been with Adele long?'

'Two—two years, *monsieur*,' responded Rebecca reluctantly, wishing he would go.

He frowned again. 'Two years. A long time, *mademoiselle*. I should imagine my sister-in-law is not the most understanding of patients. And working here—in Fiji—do you not find it lonely? Or have you friends?'

Rebecca objected to this intent questioning, but as she had no idea what his involvement with Adele might be she could hardly be rude to him. 'I—I am quite happy, thank you, *monsieur*.'

His dark eyes narrowed with mockery. 'So formal, *mademoiselle*. I am embarrassing you, I can see it. I am sorry. You must put my curiosity down to a mere male's insensitivity. I must apologise again.'

'That's not necessary, *monsieur*.' Rebecca shivered involuntarily.

At once he was contrite. 'You are cold, *mademoiselle*. I will go and contain my curiosity until another day. *Au revoir*.'

Rebecca's cheeks burned. She could have said she was far from cold. She could have said that the shiver she had experienced was stimulated by entirely different sensations. But she said nothing, and with a faint smile he stepped outside again.

Rebecca waited until he had taken several steps and then she closed the door behind him, thrusting home the bolt with trembling fingers and leaning back against the cool panels. As she pressed herself against the wood she heard the sound of a powerful engine roar to life, and a few moments later the sound died away along the private track that led to the main road. Only then did she allow herself to relax completely, but the legs on which she walked back to her bedroom were uncomfortably unsteady...

Adele St. Cloud was a woman in her late thirties who looked years older. Born with a heart complaint that had crippled her life and to some extent her mind, she had left England more than ten years ago to make her home in the warmer climate of the south Pacific, taking with her an elderly servant who had served her as both nanny and nurse. Adele's family were wealthy cloth manufacturers of French descent, living in Somerset, but apart from accepting an allowance as her due she had never got on with them. Maybe her congenital weakness was to blame, or maybe she was just naturally averse to her sisters, in any event when her only remaining parent died she lost no time in making a new life for herself in Fiji. Unfortunately her elderly nurse died some eight years later and in consequence Adele had to advertise for a replacement. And that was how Rebecca came to apply. Looking back on it now, Rebecca wondered whether she would ever have had the courage to travel so far alone if she herself had not wanted to escape from an unhappy situation.

The morning following the visit of the stranger, Rebecca was very thoughtful as she went for her early morning swim. This was the time of day she liked best when she could cast herself into the creaming waters of the lagoon and pretend the day ahead of her would not be filled with the constant demands of a fractious, unhappy woman.

As usual the water was still warm from the heat of the previous day but refreshing at this early hour. Rebecca shed her towelling jacket and ran into the water. In a white bikini, her skin tanned an even brown, she looked young and healthy, and she knew she had a lot to be thankful for. She swam strongly out to where the water deepened to dappled green and turning on to her back floated for a while, her hair spread like seaweed around her. Her eyes surveyed the shoreline, the darkness of the palms casting patches of shade in an oasis of gold. This was her particular sanctuary, for no one ever came here. The beach belonged to the villa, and as Adele never used it Rebecca had come to regard it as her own. The only sounds were the cries of the seabirds wheeling overhead and the distant thunder of the breakers over the coral reef.

When she returned to the villa she felt completely relaxed and ready to face the day and after breakfasting in the kitchen with Rosa, the Fijian housekeeper, she collected Adele's tray and went to wake her.

Adele was already awake when Rebecca went into her room. Lounging back against the silk-covered pillows she looked pale and languid. Her naturally fair colouring was given an artificial brittleness by the coarse brilliance of her hair which she persisted in bleaching and without make-up her skin was unhealthily white. Rebecca, seeing her like this, could not help but feel pity for her even though she knew that Adele would not appreciate such sentiments.

'Good morning, Miss St. Cloud,' Rebecca said now, crossing cheerfully to the bed and placing the tray across Adele's knees. 'Did you have a good night?'

Adele sniffed, regarding her nurse contemptuously. 'No, I slept badly,' she said, lifting the lid of the coffee pot and peering inside. 'Those new tablets Dr. Manson gave me are not as good as the others. It took me hours to get to sleep and then I tossed and turned——'

'You tossed and turned for hours?' Rebecca frowned rather resignedly. 'You surprise me, Miss St. Cloud. I thought you must have gone straight to sleep. After all, you didn't hear the bell, did you?'

'Bell? What bell? The telephone bell?'

Rebecca shook her head. 'The door bell.'

Adele's brows drew together. 'We had a visitor last evening?'

'Yes. Just after you had gone to—bed.'

Adele snapped her fingers. 'Stop baiting me, miss! If I didn't hear the door bell it must have been because I happened to be dozing at the moment it rang. Go on! Go on! Who was the caller? Dr. Manson? Or old Blackwell?'

'No, it wasn't the doctor, or Mr. Blackwell,' replied Rebecca, tempted to tease her employer for just a few moments longer. But then she capitulated, and said: 'It was a man. His name was Monsieur St. Clair. Does that mean anything to you?'

'Piers St. Clair?'

'He didn't tell me his Christian name, Miss St. Cloud,' replied Rebecca, suddenly aware of the similarity between the two surnames.

Adele sighed, shaking her head. 'It will be Piers,' she said, with definition. 'I know his business takes him all over the world. It is not beyond the realms of possibility that he has business here in Suva.' Her gaze grew speculative. 'Why didn't you let me know he was here?'

Rebecca sighed. 'You know Dr. Manson's instructions are very explicit. You must not be disturbed——'

'Rubbish! How dare you send away a friend when he takes the trouble to come out here to see me!'

Rebecca bit her lip. 'I didn't exactly send him away, Miss St. Cloud. He went of his own accord. He realised it was an inconvenient hour——'

Adele moved impatiently, almost upsetting her breakfast tray in the process. 'Did he say he would come back?'

'Yes,' Rebecca nodded. 'At least—I assumed——' She halted abruptly, remembering certain parts of that encounter. 'I'm—I'm sure he will come back.'

Adele's face was contorted with anger. 'Stupid girl! Can't you do anything right? Haven't you the sense to realise when a visitor might be admitted and when he might not? Surely it crossed your limited intelligence that Piers St. Clair was no ordinary visitor!'

Rebecca suffered Adele's rage in silence. Apart from the fact that to argue with her would stimulate her still further, she knew that to do so was useless. It was far better to allow her employer to rid herself of the pent-up emotions which seemed to develop so quickly these days, and afterwards go on as though nothing had happened.

Adele finally lay back on her pillows, spent, and Rebecca came forward and poured her a cup of coffee without saying a word. Adele raised the cup to her lips and after swallowing several mouthsful, she said in quite a different tone: 'What did you think of him anyway, Rebecca?'

Rebecca straightened, and sighed. She had half-hoped the subject of Piers St. Clair might be put aside for the time being. But knowing Adele she guessed she intended to make the most of the incident.

'He—he seemed very nice,' she responded rather inadequately. 'Would you like me to butter you a roll? Would you like some of this mandarin jelly?'

Adele's eyes flickered upward, and she studied her nurse's face rather mockingly. 'He's a very rich man, Rebecca. He owns several construction companies in France and Spain.'

'Indeed!' Rebecca smiled with what she hoped was a politely interested manner. 'Are you going to get up this morning? Shall I run your bath?'

Adele uttered an exclamation. 'For heaven's sake, Rebecca, stop behaving like an automaton! I asked you what you think of St. Clair. Surely you have some opinion!'

'I don't know him well enough to form any opinion, Miss St. Cloud.' Rebecca folded her hands with resignation.

'Oh, come now, Rebecca. Surely he has not changed so much over the years. He always was a handsome devil!'

'The relative attractiveness of your visitors is nothing to do with me, Miss St. Cloud,' answered Rebecca, rather shortly. 'Is there anything else you want at the moment, Miss St. Cloud——'

Adele put down her coffee cup with a clatter. 'You're deliberately misunderstanding me, miss! I just thought we might have a friendly chat about a man whom I once knew rather well ...' Her voice trailed away and there was a rather absent look on her face now. Then she seemed to realise she was being a little too confiding, for she thrust the tray aside, and said: 'Of course I'm getting up this morning. I must look my best. St. Clair will call again. I'm sure of it!'

Later in the morning, Rebecca was wheeling Adele about the spacious garden of the villa when they heard the sound of a car's engine. Adele looked up at her nurse, and her eyes brightened considerably. 'That is St. Clair,' she said. 'Come! Wheel me round to the drive. Quickly!'

Straightening her shoulders, Rebecca complied, glancing down at her uniform to make sure it was smooth and uncreased. She wore a simple navy blue uniform dress, omitting the white cap and apron on Adele's instructions. Her employer did not like to be continually reminded that she was an invalid.

A dark blue convertible stood on the drive, and even as they approached a man slid out from behind the driving wheel and looked swiftly up at the windows of the villa. Then, glancing round, he saw them, and began to walk towards them. In close-fitting beige slacks and a dark brown knitted shirt, open at the throat to reveal the brown column of his throat, Piers St. Clair was every bit as arrogantly attractive as Rebecca remembered, and she was annoyed to feel her pulse quicken. He was, after all, not the first attractive man she had known.

Adele's manner became animated as they neared him, and holding out both hands she exclaimed: 'Piers! Piers St. Clair! What in heaven's name brings you to Fiji?'

Piers St. Clair grasped her thin hands within his two strong ones and the smile he gave her was warm and enveloping. 'It is obvious you do not consider yourself a sufficient reason, Adele,' he murmured, his accent giving his voice a husky tenor. His eyes flickered for a moment over the slim figure who stood just behind her chair. 'Did your efficient Nurse Lindsay tell you that I called last evening?'

Adele nodded. 'Of course she did. I was most annoyed that she had not bothered to tell me sooner. The doctors are fools. To be awakened one evening— such a special evening—would not have harmed me.'

Piers straightened, releasing her hands. '*Chérie*, doctors must be obeyed or there is no point in consulting them, you would agree, Nurse Lindsay?' He looked fully at Rebecca.

'Of course.' Rebecca's fingers tightened on the handle of the wheelchair.

Adele glanced round at her impatiently. 'You would say that, naturally,' she said shortly. Then she looked back at Piers. 'Seriously, why are you in Fiji? Is—is everything all right at home?'

Piers lifted his shoulders in an eloquent gesture. 'As right as it will ever be,' he remarked enigmatically. Then he glanced with interest round the expanse of gardens, colourful now in the blaze of the sun. 'You have a beautiful home here, Adele. I have long been curious about it.' He thrust his hands into his trousers' pockets. 'As to what brought me here—there are plans to open up a stretch of coastline in the Yasawas. A community project, with hotels, etc. I am here to take what you would call—a survey, *oui*?'

'Ah!' Adele nodded. 'Are you here for long?'

'Two weeks, three maybe. I am staying in Suva at the moment, but I intend to move to Lautoka when my talks with government officials are concluded.'

Adele gestured towards the villa. 'Come! We will go into the house. Rose will provide us with some coffee. You'll stay to lunch, of course.'

Piers glanced once more at Rebecca, but she did not meet his eyes, and dropping his gaze to Adele, he said: 'I should like that very much.'

As they moved towards the villa, he gently but firmly took the handle of the chair from Rebecca, propelling Adele himself, and she glanced round at him warmly. Rebecca had, perforce, to walk by his side, and looking at her again he said: 'It is a beautiful morning, is it not, *mademoiselle*?'

Rebecca managed a faint smile. 'Beautiful,' she agreed. 'But then most mornings are beautiful in Fiji.'

He inclined his head in agreement and went on: 'Even so. But it puzzles me that a girl like yourself should be content with a position of this kind. My apologies to you, Adéle, but you must admit it is usually older women who take up private nursing, is it not?'

Rebecca saw Adele's impatience rise in a flood of colour up her cheeks. 'For heaven's sake, Piers!' she exclaimed. 'Don't say that! You'll make Rebecca discontented. I can assure you she is more than adequately reimbursed for her services!'

Rebecca flushed now, with embarrassment, but Piers St. Clair merely regarded her rather mockingly. 'I am sure Nurse Lindsay would not be impressed by anything I said,' he commented softly. 'She strikes me as being a very self-contained young woman.'

Adele's temper subsided, and she glanced at Rebecca with mocking amusement. 'And you would know, of course, Piers,' she said, making Rebecca feel worse than ever. She was relieved when they reached the slope leading into the villa which Adele had had installed to give her wheelchair easy access to the house.

In the hall, Rebecca halted uncertainly, and Adele said: 'Ask Rosa to bring coffee to the lounge. You can tell her we have a guest for lunch, too.'

'Yes, Miss St. Cloud.' Rebecca was willing and eager to escape, not only from Adele's mockery, but from the speculative amusement in Piers St. Clair's eyes.

For the rest of the morning she busied herself with attending to writing up her daily report and checking the contents of the medicine cupboard in Adele's bathroom. Then she tidied her room, washed a few of her personal items, and washed and added a touch of lipstick ready for lunch. As she brushed her hair into a smooth chignon on the nape of her neck, she wondered with dismay whether she would be expected to eat with her employer and her guest today. In the normal way, Adele was glad of her company, but perhaps today she would be dismissed. She hoped so; she had no liking for becoming a whipping boy for Adele's complaints and her twisted sense of humour. She sat for a

15

long moment staring at the contours of her face with critical evaluation. She was long accustomed to her features, and while she knew they presented a pleasing aspect, she had never felt any sense of complacency in the realisation. As for her hair, it would have been much easier to manage in a short style, but she was loath to have it cut. To do so would bring back too many memories of the days when she had lived with her ageing grandmother, who, while caring for her adequately, had nevertheless missed out on affection, and to save time and trouble had kept Rebecca's hair in a kind of urchin style until she was old enough to look after it herself. Those were days Rebecca had little desire to recall, days when the hapless situation her mother had found herself in seemed to be branded upon her daughter, days when her grandmother had lost no opportunity to tell her how fortunate she was not to have been abandoned in some children's home. And yet now, from the maturity of years, Rebecca could see that such a predicament might have been less tortuous in the long run.

Thrusting these thoughts aside, she rose from her dressing-table stool and crossed the bedroom to the door. Down the hall, the lounge door stood wide and she was forced to look inside to find her employer. Adele was seated in an armchair now, sipping a glass of iced cordial, while Piers St. Clair stood before the broad stone hearth, one hand resting on the mantel as he drank from a glass containing an amber-coloured liquid which Rebecca assumed was whisky. Adele looked across at her as she hovered uncertainly by the door, and said:

'Come in, come in, girl. Is lunch ready yet?'

Rebecca compressed her lips. 'I—I don't know. I—I just wanted to see if you had everything you needed. As you have Monsièur St. Clair here for lunch today, I'll—I'll eat in my room.'

Adele frowned. 'Very well, Rebecca. You may tell

16

Rosa we are ready when she is——'

'Oh, but surely Nurse Lindsay is welcome to eat with us if that is her normal practice,' exclaimed Piers St. Clair, at once. He looked at Adele. 'Our conversation is not confidential. I think we have had plenty of time for confidences, do not you, *chérie*?'

Adele raised her eyebrows. 'Rebecca can make up her own mind,' she said, with a shrug. 'We usually are alone. This situation does not normally occur.'

'I gathered that. That is why...' He spread his hands in a continental gesture.

Rebecca managed to remain calm. 'Thank you all the same, Miss St. Cloud, but I shall be quite happy to eat in my room.'

Adele's expression altered and she looked at Rebecca rather curiously, sensing that her nurse did not want to join them for lunch. In consequence, she chose to be difficult, and Rebecca, watching the changing features, felt a sense of dismay. She should have known better than to express any preference. She knew of old Adele's delight in thwarting her.

'Why don't you want to join us for lunch, Rebecca? she enquired challengingly. 'I gather you don't, do you?'

Rebecca sighed. 'My reasons are quite simple, Miss St. Cloud. I naturally assumed you and your—your guest—would prefer to be alone.'

Adele studied her lacquered fingernails. 'Now why should you imagine that, Rebecca? Do you suppose that Piers and I cherish some long-lost affection for one another? Do you think perhaps we were once lovers?'

Rebecca's cheeks burned. 'I—I'll go and tell Rosa you are ready, Miss St. Cloud.' She would not argue with her.

Adele chewed her lower lip impatiently. 'Why do you persist in disregarding my questions, Rebecca?' she exclaimed. 'Am I a child to be humoured but never debated with?'

Rebecca heaved a sigh. She cast a fleeting glance in Piers St. Clair's direction but looked away from the mockery in his gaze. Obviously he could not—or would not—help her.

'I think it would be as well if I got on with my work, Miss St. Cloud,' she said at last. 'I'm sorry if you feel I am being deliberately obtuse, but it is not part of my duties to share my—my breaks—with you.'

'You impudent little chit!' Adele stared at her incredulously. Rebecca had never answered her back in this manner before.

'Now, Adele,' murmured Piers St. Clair quietly. 'Perhaps Nurse Lindsay is right. Perhaps she does not have to spend all her time with us—with you! She has feelings, too, you know, and I think you have teased her long enough, *oui*?'

Rebecca stared at him now. Although she hated to admit it, his intervention was welcome, and his deliberate use of the verb to tease reduced it all to a playful confrontation and gave Adele the chance to get out of the situation without loss of face. In consequence, after a moment's soul-searching, Adele accepted his directions, and said reluctantly:

'Yes, that's all right, Rebecca. You can go.'

With relief, Rebecca left the room, and after informing Rosa that her employer and her guest were ready for their meal, carried a solitary tray to her room.

When the meal was over, another problem presented itself. Adele usually slept for an hour after lunch, but how was Rebecca to arrange such a thing today? She wondered whether she should simply forget her instructions, but somehow her code of training was too strong, and therefore it was with an immense sense of relief that she heard, a few moments later, the sound of a car's engine being started. She rushed to the window and looked out. Her room was on the side of the house, but by opening her window she could look out and see the further length of the drive. She was in time to see the blue convertible approach the gates and after slowing, accelerate into the road beyond.

She heaved a sigh, resting her elbows on the window ledge. So he had gone. And now she could go and settle Adele down for her sleep without complications.

But that was easier said than done. Adele was emotionally and physically stimulated by her visitor, and was in no mood to be amenable with Rebecca.

'How—how dare you speak to me like that in front of a guest!' she stormed, as soon as Rebecca appeared to take her for her rest. 'Don't imagine because Piers chose to champion you that I have forgotten it! A chit like you who doesn't even know who her own father was!'

Rebecca controlled the angry retort that sprang to her lips. Once, in a moment of compassion for Adele, she had confided the circumstances of her birth to her employer and she had regretted it ever since. 'My father was killed on his way to the church to marry my mother!' she said, through taut lips. 'I wish you would not speak to me about it again!'

'I'll bet you do!' jeered Adele unkindly. 'If your parents were such paragons of virtue, how did you come to be here?'

Rebecca flushed hotly. 'They were young—and in love! I couldn't expect you to understand that!' She turned away abruptly, unable to prevent the lump that filled her throat when she thought of the agony her mother had suffered. Her grandmother had never understood either, and had taken every opportunity to deride her for it. The train crash which had robbed her mother of her life must have seemed a blessed release.

Adele seemed to sense that she had said enough, for almost conversationally now, she said: 'It was quite nice, wasn't it? Having a man dine with us? There's the doctor, and old Blackwell, of course, but they're not the same, are they?' Andrew Blackwell was the local churchman, and although Adele was not particularly religious and grumbled about him continually, she was often glad of his company.

Rebecca composed herself and turned to help Adele into her wheelchair. Adele looked at her critically before saying: 'Seriously, why didn't you want to have lunch with us?' She frowned. 'You couldn't have thought we wanted to be alone. Piers wouldn't be interested in an old hag like me!'

'You're neither old, nor a hag,' responded Rebecca quietly. 'Don't be silly.'

Adele sighed. 'Once Piers and I knew each other very well. When I was younger and not paralysed as I am now. I used to be able to do a lot of things.'

'You're not paralysed now, Miss St. Cloud,' Rebecca contradicted her gently.

'Not actually, perhaps. But in every way that matters, I am. Tied to a wheelchair, unable to walk, or dance, or swim!' Her face twisted bitterly, and Rebecca felt distressed. It was at times like this when she felt an immense sense of compassion for Adele.

'Now then,' she said, smiling a little. 'You're not tied to the villa. We have the car. We could drive to Navua tomorrow if you like. Dr. Manson says the trip up river from there is quite beautiful. Forests and waterfalls—and it would be refreshing on the water.'

Adele turned to her impatiently. 'I don't want to go on a river trip,' she snapped. 'Don't humour me, Rebecca. I don't want that. Just because you're young and healthy, don't try to fool me! I'm useless! A wreck of a woman, not even fit to be called a woman.'

'That's nonsense!'

'What is nonsense?' Adele clenched her fists. 'Do you think I don't notice the way men look at *you*? The way Dr. Manson looks at you. The way *Piers* looked at you!'

Rebecca's cheeks were scarlet. 'Please, Miss St.

Cloud——' she began.

'Why? Why shouldn't I say it? It's true, isn't it?' Adele's eyes narrowed. 'And you can't fool me about that, either, Rebecca! Piers was the reason you didn't want to lunch with me. Piers! I wonder why? What did he say to you last evening to cause you such anxiety?'

Rebecca began to wheel the chair into the corridor and from there to Adele's room, but Adele was not finished yet. Twisting in her seat, she watched her nurse's mobile face, and her own grew contemptuous. Turning round again, she went silent, and Rebecca was relieved. But as they reached Adele's bedroom, Adele spoke again, this time in an entirely different voice.

'Tell me, Rebecca, now you've had the chance to speak to him again, what do you think of Piers?'

Rebecca bit her lip. What did Adele want of her now? Searching for a suitable reply, she said: 'He seems—quite nice.' She helped Adele on to the bed and began to loosen the buttons of her dress. 'Have you known him long?'

'Most of my life,' answered Adele, sliding her arms out of the dress. "His family and mine were always very close.'

'I see.' Rebecca bent to unfasten Adele's shoes and Adele's eyes narrowed.

'At one time—it was thought that he and I—might marry,' she said.

Rebecca looked up, hiding her surprise. But then, of course, Piers St. Clair would be about Adele's own age. Something he had said came back to her: he had called her his sister-in-law! A strange feeling twisted her stomach. He was married, then. Married to Adele's sister.

Adele watched Rebecca closely. 'Why are you frowning?' she asked. 'Are you so shocked by that knowledge?'

'Why, no!' Rebecca answered quickly. 'But—it was

something Monsieur St. Clair said.'

'Which was?' Adele prompted.

Rebecca shrugged. 'Only that he was your brother-in-law.'

Adele nodded, and lay back against the pillows. 'That's right.' Her mouth twisted again. 'He married one of my four sisters.'

Rebecca straightened, lifting Adele's legs on to the bed. 'So he's married,' she said, rather flatly.

Adele regarded her intently, and then a strange smile curved her thin lips. 'My sister died,' she said, closing her eyes.

Rebecca pressed a hand to her stomach. 'I'll get the sedative,' she said.

Adele's eyes flickered. 'That won't be necessary, Rebecca. I feel—very tired.'

Rebecca hesitated. Adele's cheeks were still flushed with hectic colour, but she could not force her to take the capsule.

'Very well,' she said now, 'I'll leave you. But if you want anything, just call.'

'I will.' Adele closed her eyes again. 'By the way, Piers is coming for dinner tomorrow evening. Do you think you could ask Rosa to use a little more imagination with the food than she usually does?'

Rebecca walked to the door. 'I'll speak to her,' she agreed, and went quickly out of the room.

CHAPTER TWO

THE next morning Rebecca went down to the beach as usual to take her early morning swim. A faint mist cast gauzy nets across the horizon heralding another perfect day. Spiders' webs among the palms were hung with dew which sparkled like diamonds, and the sand underfoot was cool and soft between her toes. Shedding her towelling jacket, she stood for a moment, poised on the shoreline, stretching her arms to the rays of the rising sun.

And so it was, silhouetted against the golden skyline, that the man saw her as he emerged from the trees and came walking panther-like along the sand towards her. As though suddenly conscious of the approach of an intruder, Rebecca swung round and gasped, as much with annoyance as with surprise, as she recognised the interloper.

'*Bonjour, mademoiselle*,' Piers St. Clair said casually, reaching her side. 'Do you usually swim at this hour?'

Rebecca managed to control her colour. This man always seemed to put her at a disadvantage, and dressed only in a bikini, her feet bare, she felt somehow aware and vulnerable.

'This is the only time of day I can call my own,' she replied, rather pointedly. 'Miss St. Cloud does not rise until nine—or thereabouts.'

'Ah, I see,' Piers nodded.

Rebecca hesitated, and then said: 'I understood you were invited for dinner—not for breakfast.'

He smiled. 'What a sharp little tongue you have, *mademoiselle*. It may surprise you to know that I did not intend calling at the villa. My hotel room was hot and I was not tired. I decided to drive for a while and as I passed Adele's villa I saw you crossing the lawns towards the beach. I apologise if my arrival is something of an intrusion.'

Rebecca coloured now. He had successfully reduced her small attempt at sarcasm to mere pettiness. With an inconsequent shrug of her shoulders, she said: 'As you are a friend—a relative, almost—of my employer, your presence on the beach could hardly be termed an intrusion when I am merely Adele's employee.' She bit her lip. She had not meant to say Adele, it had just slipped out, but she was just as sure that he had noticed it.

Piers St. Clair frowned. 'I care less and less for your explanations, *mademoiselle*,' he commented dryly. 'As I have said, I did not intend coming here. I should not have.'

With a flick of his fingers against his dark trousers, he turned and walked away along the beach, and Rebecca pressed her lips together unhappily. For all she was sure he would not mention this incident to Adele, nevertheless she felt a sense of shame that she should have behaved so rudely. After all, it was not his fault that she found him disturbingly attractive. No doubt he was used to women finding him so. It was just that some inner sense warned her about becoming involved with him, without taking into account the fact that he might not feel attracted to her. Sighing indecisively, she stepped forward into the water, allowing the small waves to ripple round her ankles. She would not allow thoughts of him to mar these moments of the day. This was the time when she shed all the petty restrictions Adele imposed and became a sun-worshipper.

The water was delicious, and it creamed over her shoulders delightfully. There was a sensuousness about warm water that compared with nothing she had ever known back in England. Occasionally, late in the evening, when Adele was fast asleep, she came and swam without her bikini, but although this beach was private she would not dare to do so in daylight. Piers St. Clair's unexpected arrival was indicative of what could happen.

Later in the morning Adele received a telephone call, and when she put down the receiver her face was hard and angry. 'That was Piers,' she said shortly, as Rebecca turned from arranging some flowers in a huge urn in the hall. 'He has postponed our dinner engagement.'

Rebecca swallowed hard, forcing her face to remain composed. 'Oh! Has he?' she murmured quietly. 'Did —did he say why?'

Adele chewed her lower lip. 'Something to do with his business here, I believe,' she snapped moodily, her manner denoting the kind of day Rebecca might expect from now on. 'In any event, he's not coming! Damn him!'

Rebecca couldn't help but feel relieved, even though a small core of anxiety inside her told her that his reasons for rejecting Adele's invitation were not wholly impersonal. But she successfully hid her own feelings and managed to put all thoughts of Piers St. Clair to the back of her mind.

It was three days before she saw him again. Although Adele expected a telephone call daily, none came, and Rebecca was beginning to believe that he did not intend returning to the villa at all. When his business in Suva was over and he went to Lautoka the chances of seeing him were much less obvious and she told herself she was relieved.

Even so, she could not deny that his intervention in their lives had been a disrupting influence from which it would take time to dissociate themselves. Thus it was quite a shock for Rebecca when she encountered Piers St. Clair again.

She had gone shopping in Suva for Adele, and had

completed her purchases and was idly wandering among the market stalls, when a stall selling oil of sandalwood attracted her. The oil was being sold in cut glass jars and was obviously intended to attract the eye of the tourist. The dark-skinned islander who was in charge of the stall sensed her interest at once as she stood, fingering a jar with probing curiosity, and he began to extol the virtues of the product with rolling eyes and extravagant hand gestures. Rebecca was smilingly shaking her head when she became aware that a man had come to stand slightly behind her and casually she glanced round.

Piers St. Clair inclined his head solemnly, his face dark and serious. '*Bonjour, mademoiselle,*' he murmured smoothly.

'Good morning.' Rebecca managed a faint smile, and stood the glass jar back on the stall rather jerkily.

His eyes flickered to the oil and he said: 'Are you going to buy it?'

Rebecca shook her head again. 'No, I don't think so. I—I—the glass jars caught my eye.'

'As they were intended to do. Did you know that Fijians used to use this oil to anoint their bodies? It was very highly valued in that capacity. Nowadays, less so.'

Rebecca lifted her shoulders. 'I like the fragrance.'

He raised his dark eyebrows, and then looked at the stall-holder with questioning eyes. '*Cette essence,*' he said, indicating the jar Rebecca had put down. '*Combien?*'

Rebecca stared at him uncomfortably, and then before he could say anything she moved quickly away. She had the distinct feeling that he intended buying the oil for her, and she didn't want that.

A ripple of apprehension running along her spine, she walked swiftly to the edge of the market area and waiting until the road was clear went quickly across. The noise of the traffic was deafening after the peace of the villa, and the sights and sounds of the city took some getting used to. As did the smell of dried copra that hung over the harbour on hot, humid days with intensity.

She had left the car parked in a side street. She knew the city area quite well, and had no fears for her safety among these big friendly people. From time to time she exchanged a greeting with a shopkeeper who was sitting outside his store, cross-legged in the sunshine. Many of these shopkeepers were Indians, and there was a variety of costume to be seen, from the calf-length sulus, worn by men and women alike, to the exotically draped sari, that seemed to enhance the femininity of all women, no matter what nationality. At this time of the year, too, Suva was thronged with tourists, and the tourist attractions did good business. Rebecca smiled to herself, as her surroundings temporarily banished all anxieties about Piers St. Clair, and she thought how lucky she was to live in such a paradise.

Reaching the car, she bent to unlock it, and then straightened to find the man she had been escaping from beside her. Containing her annoyance, she said: 'Are you following me?' in rather a tight little voice.

'Yes,' he said, almost negligently, and leaned against the car's bonnet, his arms folded.

Today, in navy shorts, that drew attention to the brown muscular length of his legs, and a cream silk sweater that was unbuttoned almost to his waist, he looked somehow dark and alien, yet infinitely attractive. His thick dark hair was smooth against his head, and long sideburns darkened his cheekbones, while dark eyes surveyed her with enigmatic arrogance.

Rebecca, conscious of the formality of her uniform, was glad she had worn it. Somehow it added to the composure that seemed to be deserting her as it always did when he was around. Why did he persist in disturbing her in this way? Did it amuse him to make fun of her? Or was she a novelty to a man satiated by women of his own set? Whatever his reasons it could only spell disaster for her. Now she turned to him and said:

'Exactly why are you following me, Monsieur St. Clair?'

He shrugged indolently. 'To give you this,' he said, offering her a parcel wrapped in coloured paper.

Rebecca did not take the parcel, but after putting her shopping bag into the car, put her hands behind her back. 'Thank you, but I don't want anything from you,' she asserted jerkily. 'Now—if you'll excuse me——'

Piers St. Clair regarded her coolly. 'What do you suppose is in the parcel?' he queried sharply.

Rebecca coloured. 'I'd rather not say.'

'You think it is the flagon of sandalwood oil, don't you?' he demanded.

Rebecca felt terrible. 'Well? What if I do?'

He toyed with the wrapping on the parcel. 'And what if I tell you you dropped something in the market—something I found and re-wrapped in this rather—well—colourful paper?'

Rebecca's eyes went immediately to her shopping bag. Without taking it out and checking over the contents she could not be certain she had everything she had bought. Pressing her lips together for a moment, she said: 'I'm sure I didn't drop anything, *monsieur*.' She ran a hand over her hair, checking that the chignon was secure with nervous fingers. 'I think you are deliberately baiting me, for some twisted reason of your own.'

He raised his dark eyebrows, and with a deft movement he allowed the parcel to unwind in his fingers until a container of talcum powder fell into his palm, free of the wrapping. Rebecca stared at the talcum powder with disbelieving eyes. It was the cologne-scented talc she had bought for Adele. Her eyes lifted to his, but still his were guarded, revealing nothing.

28

Rebecca swallowed hard, and then said: 'That is mine?'

'If you say so,' he remarked lightly.

Rebecca took a deep breath. 'I couldn't have dropped it without hearing it fall.'

'What? In the noise of the market area? Don't you think so, *mademoiselle*?'

Rebecca sighed. 'I'm not sure.' She ran her tongue over her upper lip. 'Perhaps you took it from my bag.'

He shook his head impatiently. 'What have I done that you have such a low opinion of me?' he questioned. 'What has my inestimable sister-in-law been telling you?'

Rebecca opened the car door wider. 'She has told me nothing, *monsieur*. Now, if you'll excuse me——'

'Don't you want your talcum powder, *mademoiselle*?'

'Oh—oh, yes, I suppose so.' Rebecca almost snatched the container from his hands and thrust it into the back of the car with the rest of her shopping. 'Now I must go. Adele—I mean Miss St. Cloud—will wonder why I've been so long.'

He gave a negligent lift of his shoulders and straightened from the car's bonnet. 'Very well, *mademoiselle*. If you insist.'

Rebecca got behind the steering wheel and then looked up at him almost appealingly. 'I—I don't understand you, *monsieur*.'

'*Non!* I would agree with you there.'

Rebecca hesitated, biting her lip. 'Are you—I mean —will you be coming to dinner before—before you leave?'

He regarded her with intense dark eyes. 'Do you want me to?' he asked softly.

Rebecca's stomach contracted. 'I—I—it's nothing to do with me,' she stammered.

'Is it not?' He shrugged. 'Yes, I will come. I will ring Adele and arrange a time.' His expression grew brood-

29

ing. 'And afterwards? Will you go for a drive with me?'

Rebecca's eyes were wide and startled. 'I—I—I am Adele's employee. I cannot make arrangements like that. Besides,' she fumbled for the ignition, 'Adele would never agree.'

'Adele need not know—need she?' His eyes held hers.

Rebecca took a rather shaky breath. 'I—I really think you—you are wasting your time, *monsieur*,' she murmured unsteadily. 'I—I am not like the—the women you know...'

'I recognise that,' he replied coolly. 'I do have some perception.'

Rebecca shook her head helplessly. 'I—I must go,' she said. 'Good—goodbye.'

'*Au revoir*,' he answered, and stepped back as she put the small saloon into gear, and drove rather erratically away.

Outside the city limits the road stretched straight for some distance, cutting between the blue waters of the Bay of Islands. It was unbelievably beautiful, but this morning Rebecca had no heart to appreciate it. She was sick and shaken, terrified at the knowledge that Piers St. Clair could exercise so much power over her. In his presence her antagonism just melted away and so might her resistance.

Even so, it was exhilarating to know that he found her attractive, and that awful traitorous part of her that responded to flattery wanted to take what he offered with both hands. But the sane part of her knew that anything he might offer would be dangerous to accept and in consequence she was torn both ways.

When she got back to the villa, Adele was resting on a lounger in the garden, shaded by a huge striped umbrella. She gave Rebecca a speculative stare, and then said: 'You've been long enough. What have you been buying?'

Rebecca managed not to blush. 'Just what you asked me to buy,' she replied, kneeling down on the warm mosaic tiles and beginning to unpack her straw shopping bag. The talc which Piers had given her was on the top and she handed this first to Adele. Then she went on through her purchases, handing out stockings and make-up, hair rollers and hairnets, toilet articles and toothpaste. At the bottom of her bag was a container of cologne-scented talc, identical to the first she had given Adele.

Taking it out, she stared at it incredulously, and Adele, seeing her consternation, exclaimed: 'For heaven's sake, girl, what have you been thinking of? Buying two tins of talc!'

Rebecca coloured now and thrust the second container aside. 'I—I bought it for myself,' she said quickly.

'But you don't like that fragrance,' said Adele impatiently. 'There's no need to pretend, Rebecca. I don't mind having two tins. They'll both get used in time.' She bent and lifted the second container from where Rebecca had put it.

Rebecca bit her lip tightly. 'Oh, but really...' she began.

Adele sniffed. 'But nothing, my girl. Go and put these things away, and then ask Rosa for some coffee.'

It was the following day before Piers St. Clair telephoned, and Rebecca spent the period between meeting him at the market and his eventual arrival for dinner in a strangely unreal sense of expectancy. She had pondered the riddle of the talc until she had realised that as her bag was made of interlaced straw it would have been quite easy for him to see what was in it. Even so, she speculated upon his perception which had instantly jumped to the conclusion she might place upon the parcel in his hand, and the subsequent trick he had played upon her. He must know her sex extremely well, she thought with a sinking heart, the incident adding to her awareness of him as a potentially dangerous man. He arranged with Adele that he should join her for dinner the following evening, and the next morning Adele insisted upon making one of her very infrequent excursions into Suva to visit her hairdresser. Rebecca was doubtful of the advisability of such an excursion on a day when Adele was bound to become over-stimulated anyway, but there was little she could do to prevent it. When Adele made up her mind, there was little anyone could do.

In the afternoon, while Adele rested, Rebecca pressed the gown she had chosen to wear that evening. Adele had been loath to allow Rosa to do it, so Rebecca had offered in order to avoid any further upheavals.

Rebecca herself was absorbed with her own thoughts, aware that she was mentally searching for reasons for being absent from the villa this evening. Not that Adele expected her to join them for dinner, indeed the question had never arisen, but somehow she wanted to put some distance between herself and her employer's brother-in-law.

She helped Adele to change after her bath, and Adele preened herself for a few moments in front of her dressing-table mirror.

'Quite nice,' she conceded at last. 'Don't you think so, Rebecca?'

Rebecca managed a smile. 'Very nice, Miss St. Cloud,' she agreed, nodding. Then she bit her lip. 'You will promise not to over-excite yourself this evening, won't you, Miss St. Cloud? This—well—this has been quite an exhausting day for you, and naturally——'

Adele stared at her. 'What are you talking about, girl? You'll be here to keep an eye on me yourself, won't you? Surely you know I expect you to join us?'

Rebecca's cheeks burned. 'Oh, no! No, Miss St. Cloud. I—I have—made other arrangements.'

'What other arrangements?' Adele's voice was sharp.

Rebecca swallowed hard, searching her mind for excuses. 'I—I thought I might go out. I—I—haven't had many evenings off——'

'And where would you go alone?' snapped Adele. 'You may have freedom of the island during the day, but after dark—that's a different matter.'

'You—you did say—I might use the car.'

'I know that. But it just so happens that I require your services this evening. Now, snap out of that awkward mood and go and get yourself changed. I don't expect you to eat dinner in your uniform.'

Rebecca stared at her employer unhappily. 'I'd prefer to eat dinner in my room, Miss St. Cloud,' she asserted clearly.

Adele's eyes flickered. 'Why? Because of Piers?'

'What? No! No.' Rebecca turned away, and in consequence did not see the narrowing of Adele's eyes.

'Well, it can't be me,' remarked the older woman mockingly. 'You've had dinner with me plenty of times.'

Rebecca gathered her composure and turned back to her. 'I would feel the same, no matter who your guest might be,' she said tautly. 'Besides, I can't recall you showing such a desire for my company before.' She frowned. 'Why do you want me to join you for dinner?'

If Adele was surprised by this sudden show of confidence, she hid it admirably, and smiling slightly said: 'Perhaps, as your days here are so uneventful, I felt sorry for you. And after all, it isn't every day you get the chance to break bread with a millionaire!'

Rebecca's nails dug into the palms of her hands. 'Do I have a choice?'

Adele's expression hardened. 'No, miss, you do not! Now go and prepare yourself, or do you want to be responsible for my over-stimulation?'

Rebecca heaved a sigh, and with a helpless gesture

left the room. In her own room she surveyed the contents of her wardrobe critically. What on earth was she going to wear? Short dresses were cooler, but somehow unsuitable in the islands when so many oriental styles were much more feminine. She drew out an all-white gown, trimmed with gold braid, its classic lines cut to ankle length. The bodice was swathed under her breasts, but otherwise it fell without fullness to her feet. With her colouring, and the tan she had acquired, it would look attractive, but did she want to look attractive? Surely she would be more sensible to wear a less arresting garment. She had no desire to arouse any further interest.

Thrusting the white gown aside, she pulled out a jungle-printed caftan. It, too, was long, but its lines were all-concealing, and the wide long sleeves hid the rounded contours of her arms.

Throwing it on the bed, she went to take a shower, and later, after she was dressed, she surveyed her appearance with approval. Certainly the colour did nothing for her, although she could wear almost anything really.

She joined Adele in the lounge just as the sound of a car could be heard drawing up outside the villa. Rosa went to answer the door and a few moments later came into the lounge and said:

'Monsieur Piers St. Clair, madam, and his companion, Mademoiselle Yvonne Dupuis!'

Rebecca could feel the colour drain out of her face as Piers came into the room, looking tall, and lean, and dark, in a white dinner jacket, a maroon handkerchief in his pocket showing a splash of colour. With him was one of the most beautiful women Rebecca had ever seen, although she was by no means young. Rebecca judged her age to be anywhere between thirty-five and forty-five, and there were strands of grey in her lustrous dark hair. Even so, she was immaculately elegant, and the slenderness of her figure owed noth-

34

ing to clever upholstering. In a gown of silver grey crepe that moulded her body lovingly, a darker grey cape across her shoulders, she looked magnificent, and Rebecca glanced swiftly at Adele to note her reactions.

But to her surprise, Adele seemed not at all perturbed, and her greeting left Rebecca in no doubt that she had expected this second guest. Rebecca herself felt confused. Exactly why had Adele made such a thing about her joining them when she had known that Piers St. Clair was bringing a guest? And why hadn't she warned Rebecca that her brother-in-law would not be alone? Rebecca compressed her lips, wondering what distorted enjoyment Adele expected to get out of this situation. Had she sensed her nurse's interest in Piers and chosen this way to show her how hopeless were any aspirations in that direction? Surely she must know that Rebecca was aware of that herself. Or did she? Either way, tonight was going to be infinitely more difficult to endure.

While Adele chattered to Yvonne Dupuis, leaving Rebecca to realise that the two women had known one another for many years, Piers, after a smiling greeting to his sister-in-law, made his way to Rebecca's side.

'*Bonsoir, mademoiselle*,' he murmured, regarding her with his intensely dark eyes. 'I wondered whether you would be permitted to join us.'

Rebecca's first instinct was to make some excuse and move away from him, but to do so would be tantamount to admitting her nervousness of him, so instead she said: 'Miss St. Cloud insisted. Unfortunately, I am not in a position to choose.'

His eyes narrowed slightly. 'Why do you persist in behaving so childishly?' he enquired, in a low tone. 'It is not becoming.'

Rebecca looked across at Adele who looked up at that moment and said: 'Shall we have a drink? Rebecca, will you get them? By the way, Yvonne, this is my nurse, Rebecca Lindsay. Rebecca, Mademoiselle

Dupuis and I were at school together.'

Adele's tone was so light and pleasant, that Rebecca had no choice but to go and shake hands with the French woman and then ask her what she would like to drink. At the cocktail cabinet, her fingers were all thumbs, and after she had dropped a small bottle of dry ginger with a disturbing clatter on the glass surface, she felt Piers join her, and take the offending bottle out of her hands.

Deftly, and without spilling a drop, Piers dealt with their individual requests, and after handing Rebecca the bitter lemon she had insisted upon having, he poured himself rather a stiff measure of brandy.

'*Cognac, mademoiselle,*' he remarked, as Rebecca watched him swirling the amber-coloured liquid round in its balloon glass. 'If ever I need it, it restores my—what would you say—*equilibre?*'

'Equilibrium,' said Rebecca, rather flatly, looking down into her own glass.

'Ah, *oui*, equilibrium!' He half smiled. 'You understand?'

Rebecca compressed her lips. 'I would not have thought anything would disturb your—equilibrium,' she replied. 'You seem superbly confident to me.'

His eyes searched her face, lingering disturbingly on her mouth for a long moment. 'But then—you do not know me very well—yet,' he commented softly.

Rebecca turned away. She would not listen to him, and as luck would have it Rosa came in at that moment to announce that dinner was served. Piers took charge of Adele's chair, making her laugh as they walked ahead of Rebecca and the French woman into the dining room.

The meal was silent for Rebecca. Round a table it was so much easier for Adele to talk equally to both her guests and in consequence Rebecca was left to herself. She didn't mind. Indeed, it was easier that way, but she longed to escape from all of them.

Coffee was served in the lounge, and the windows were thrust wide to let in the cool evening air. Mesh screens prevented the hundreds of moths and insects from penetrating to the attraction of the lamplight, and it was very pleasant to relax there. But after drinking her coffee, Rebecca rose and said:

'If you don't mind, I'll leave you now. I—I have some reports to attend to. And I have rather a headache, too.'

Adele frowned. 'Now, Rebecca,' she said impatiently, 'no report is that urgent. And as for your headache, I should think a walk round the garden would cure that. I'm sure Monsieur St. Clair would accompany you.' Her gaze rested momentarily on Piers who had risen too.

Rebecca coloured brilliantly. What was Adele trying to do? Why should she suggest that Piers St. Clair should accompany her on a walk round the garden? She had never shown any interest in her nurse's welfare before.

'Thank you, but——' she began, when Piers said: 'Adele is right. The night air would do you more good than sitting in your room. I'm sure Yvonne and Adele can find plenty to talk about.'

Yvonne leaned forward and put her hand on his arm, attracting his attention. 'Let Nurse Lindsay decide for herself, *chéri*,' she murmured insinuatively. 'She may be tired.'

Rebecca watched that interchange with reluctance. Exactly what relationship did Yvonne Dupuis have with him? From the intimacy of her expression, Rebecca could only think the worst. Seizing upon Yvonne's words, she nodded vigorously.

'Yes, that's it,' she asserted. 'I—I am tired. I'd like to go to bed.'

Adele's expression was hard. 'And what about me, young woman? You forget—your duties are not yet over for the evening.'

Rebecca hesitated. 'I'm sure Rosa wouldn't mind helping you—as she has done on those evenings when I have been out.' Only twice had she been out in the evening, and that was when Dr. Manson's wife had invited her for dinner.

Short of appearing a fractious employer, there was nothing Adele could do, and ignoring Piers' contemptuous gaze, Rebecca wished them all goodnight, and sought the comparative sanctuary of her room. She knew Adele would make her pay for thwarting her in this manner, but right now she couldn't have cared less...

CHAPTER THREE

THE following morning Rebecca did not go down to swim as usual. In the early hours she was awakened by Adele calling weakly for her and throwing on her dressing gown she hurried to her employer's room.

Adele was lying across the bed. She had obviously been to the bathroom but had collapsed on her way back and was now panting for breath, pressing a hand to her chest as though to break the pain which seemed to be tearing her apart.

Rebecca helped her on to the bed properly, and then hurried to the bathroom cabinet. A few minutes later, with the aid of a drug, and Rebecca's soothing presence, Adele began to look more normal, and Rebecca ran to telephone for Dr. Manson.

When the elderly doctor arrived he endorsed everything Rebecca had done and chided Adele for behaving so recklessly the day before. 'You should know by now that you cannot spend the whole day in a state of excitement, my dear,' he told her, shaking his head reprovingly. 'And then to eat the kind of rich food Rebecca tells me you have eaten...' He sighed. 'It's lucky you have Rebecca here. I don't know what might have happened...'

Adele, gradually recovering from the paralysing attack, gave her nurse an impatient look. 'I'm all right,' she said ungraciously. 'There was no need to call you at all. Rebecca coped with everything that was needed. She only wanted to let you know that I'd been disobedient. God! I wish I was free of this—this—dependence!'

Dr. Manson looked at her compassionately. 'Now you know as well as I do that you'll never be free,' he said quietly, 'and it's something you've got to live with, it's something you've got to accept and take into account at all times. You've lived with it long enough to know that.'

Adele's expression was bitter. 'I've lived with it all my life!' she exclaimed, in a tortured voice.

Dr. Manson turned away, looking helplessly at Rebecca, and Rebecca gave an imperceptible nod of her head. They were both aware of the dangers of the depression Adele was sinking into now that the attack was over.

After the doctor had gone, Rebecca gave Adele a sedative. The older woman objected, but Rebecca used the hypodermic and presently Adele closed her eyes and gave in to the inertia that was creeping over her. After she was asleep, Rebecca cleared the room, tidying away the garments which Rosa had left about the floor. In all honesty, she felt a terrible sense of guilt about the whole affair. Maybe she should have stayed up. Maybe she should have seen Adele into bed herself. Maybe she would have noticed the tell-tale signs that heralded an attack.

So many maybes, and none of them certain. Adele had seemed perfectly all right all evening, and might have been perfectly all right all night, too, if she had not got up to go to the bathroom. No doubt the rich food and the small quantity of drink she had consumed had been responsible for that little journey.

Sighing, she left the bedroom and went to her own room to get dressed. It was already after seven and there was no point in going back to bed. Adele might need her.

When she was dressed she went to the kitchen and begged some coffee from Rosa. The dark-skinned housekeeper looked anxious and asked troubled questions about her employer. Rebecca reassured her, and then said:

'Did she seem all right when you put her to bed last night?'

Rosa considered. 'I think so, miss. She wasn't flushed or anything. Just tired, that's all. I saw that she took her tablet like you told me, miss, and she seemed fine!'

Rebecca smiled. 'That's okay, Rosa. Don't worry any more. She's going to be as awkward as usual in a day or two. But she'll have to stay in bed for today and possibly tomorrow, too. Dr. Manson said so.'

'Yes, miss.' Rosa handed her a mug of steamingly aromatic coffee. 'Are you recovered this morning? Monsieur St. Clair told me you had a headache and had gone to bed.'

Rebecca coloured. 'Monsieur St. Clair? When did you see him?'

'He helped me to put Adele to bed before they left, miss.'

'Oh! Oh, I see.' Rebecca bit her lip. 'Were they late in leaving?' She had not heard the car, but possibly that was because her room was away from the drive.

'Not very, miss. Soon after you went to bed really.'

Rebecca nodded, and taking the coffee she walked to the wide kitchen windows which looked out on the tropical plantation-like growth which encroached almost to the lawn at the back of the house. There was a bitter-sweet ache inside her which could not be denied. Why did Piers St. Clair affect her like this? Why couldn't she just put him out of her mind altogether?

Adele's unexpected illness at least prevented her from exerting too much effort in her condemnation of Rebecca's actions on the night of the dinner party. When she was fit enough to talk normally towards the end of the following day she merely contented herself with some sneering comments about Rebecca's inadequacy, and Piers St. Clair's name was not mentioned. Even so, Rebecca had the distinct impression that Adele chose not to bring his name into it for some devious reasons of her own, and she wished she knew a little more of what her employer was thinking.

Adele objected strongly to having to stay in bed, but perhaps the attack had served a purpose in that it had made her a little more chary of disobeying her doctor's instructions, and she remained where she was. Rebecca's job was a little harder in consequence, as she had to do everything for her, including giving her a blanket bath, and although Adele was thin her bones were heavy and required all Rebecca's strength to lift her.

By the evening of the second day after the attack, Adele seemed almost normal, and Rebecca took the opportunity to go down for a swim after she had settled her employer down for the night. It was the first opportunity she had had to leave the villa, for the previous evening she had been too conscious of the possible dangers of a second attack.

It was a beautiful evening, and Rebecca put on her white bikini and her beach jacket, and ran eagerly across the grass and down the slope to the beach. The air was soft and velvety, and the sky above was a dome of midnight blue studded with diamonds.

Shedding the beach jacket, she allowed the wavelets to ripple round her toes, their chill wholly welcoming after the heat of the day. Then she plunged into the water, and swam strongly out to where she could no longer reach the bottom with her toes. Her limbs felt revitalised as the damp heat of the day was washed away, and she spread her legs and floated, staring up into the arc of sky above.

When she swam back to the shore, she felt cool and refreshed, and shedding her wet bikini she put on the beach jacket, wrapping it closely about her. But even as she did so, she heard the sound of a twig being trampled underfoot, and she swung round in startled expectation. The figure of a man emerged from the shadows of the palms, and her first instinct was to run, but although she was trembling, she stood her ground.

'Are you aware that you are trespassing?' she enquired, summoning all her confidence. 'This is a private beach!'

'And you are crazy bathing here alone!' snapped a husky voice, with an unmistakable accent. '*Mon Dieu*, Rebecca, have you no sense?'

Rebecca stared up at Piers St. Clair with mutinous eyes. 'Have—have you been spying on me?' she asked tremulously.

Piers uttered an exclamation in his own language. 'Of course I have not been "spying" on you. I admit I came here in the hope that I might see you, but the sight of the naked female frame is no novelty to me!' His tone was hard and angry. 'God in heaven, Rebecca, what would you have done if I had been an intruder? Do you imagine you could offer any defence, dressed like that?'

'This—this is a private beach,' she said again, shakily.

'But it is not sealed off, is it?' Piers raised his eyes skyward. 'You constantly enrage me! When I speak to you—when I attempt to be friendly with you, you turn on me like a—a—she-cat! Yet you come here, alone, without taking any precautions for your own safety!' He snapped his fingers angrily. 'I—I lose patience with you!'

'I don't—recall asking for your indulgence!' said Rebecca shortly. 'Now, if you'll stand out of my way——'

Piers stood still, staring down at her, and when she moved to walk round him, he moved also, blocking her path. Rebecca looked up at him angrily, using her anger as a shield against his undoubted attraction.

'Please!' she said tightly. 'Get out of my way!'

Piers stared at her for a long moment, and then without a word, stepped out of her path. The relief was such that Rebecca found it incredibly difficult to move at all. But at last, on rather stiff legs, she walked up the beach and crossed the grass to the villa. She didn't look back, but she was aware of his eyes upon her the whole of the way.

The next few days passed uneventfully. Adele improved considerably and was able to get up and about again. Rebecca knew she had had a telephone call from Piers, but what he had said she was not to know. Later in the week, Adele deemed it necessary to inform her that her brother-in-law had gone to Lautoka, but if she expected some reaction from Rebecca she was disappointed. Rebecca had schooled herself not to show any emotion, and consequently Adele soon grew tired of baiting her.

At the end of the week, Rebecca surprised Adele making a telephone call herself; surprised because Adele always had Rebecca get her calls for her. However, as Adele obviously wanted privacy, Rebecca left her, but she could not help wondering who she had been calling so secretly.

Two afternoons later, after Rebecca had settled Adele down for her nap, Piers St. Clair made another appearance. He came walking into the wide tiled hall, just as Rebecca was gathering the dead flowers from their vases preparatory to adding new ones. In cream pants and a navy silk shirt that hung open, he looked cool and dark, while Rebecca, in her high collared uniform dress, was feeling the heat of the day.

'Oh,' she said, when she saw him. 'I—I didn't hear the car.'

He shrugged. 'I left it outside the drive. I guessed Adele might be asleep and I didn't want to disturb her.'

Rebecca began to wrap up the dead flowers in an old newspaper she had brought for the purpose. 'If you knew Adele would be asleep, why have you come?' she asked, rather unevenly.

His eyes darkened. 'For obvious reasons. Look, Rebecca, I can imagine what Adele has told you about me, but please, don't judge me so hastily!'

Rebecca stared at him. 'It's not my prerogative to

44

judge anyone, Monsieur St. Clair,' she said tautly. 'I just feel that—well—you're wasting your time, and your undoubted talents, on me!'

'Be silent!' His voice was harsh. 'You know absolutely nothing of life—of *my* life!' He clenched his fists angrily. 'Rebecca,' his tone changed, 'get ready, and I will take you for a drive, *oui*?'

Rebecca took a deep breath. 'I couldn't do that, *monsieur*. Miss St. Cloud might need me.'

'Not for an hour at least,' he said huskily. 'Is it so much to ask? Is my company so abhorrent to you?'

She turned away. All her senses cried out for her to accept; only common sense said no. But sometimes common sense must be overruled for the sake of sanity, and Rebecca moved towards the corridor which led to her room.

'Well?' he demanded fiercely.

'I'll get ready,' she murmured reluctantly, and left him.

When she came back he was pacing the hall impatiently, like a caged animal, but his eyes brightened when he saw her. In a short white pleated skirt and a sleeveless ribbed sweater she looked quite lovely.

'I've told Rosa we're going out, just in case Adele wakes,' he said, indicating that she should precede him out of the villa.

Rebecca nodded, and they walked down the drive together. At its foot, the dark blue convertible was parked, and Piers helped her inside before walking round the bonnet and sliding in beside her. His thigh brushed hers and she looked at him quickly before looking away again.

They drove north from the villa, taking the road into the hinterland which was still largely uncultivated and scarcely inhabited. Here the jungle ran riot, and at times the road itself was lost beneath the snaking creepers of the parasites that wound themselves in a death spiral round the trunks of the trees in the rain forest at the head of the valley. The atmosphere was moist and sometimes unpleasantly aromatic with decaying vegetation. Rebecca lay back in her seat and wondered with mild curiosity exactly where they were going.

It wasn't until they had been travelling for almost three-quarters of an hour that she realised that wherever it was they were going was far too far to attempt in such a limited time. The silence that had stretched between them since they began their journey was such that she was loath to break it, but as it happened she did not have to.

They had been climbing for some time, up through the rain forest, but now they emerged on a plateau which gave a magnificent view of the whole valley, and where, amazingly, a waterfall fell in solitary splendour from some few feet above them away down the rocky slope.

Piers brought the car to a halt and opening his door he slid out. Hands on hips, he surveyed the panorama of the island spread out below him and then turned to look at Rebecca, still seated in the car. '*Bien?*' he said challengingly. 'Magnificent, is it not?'

'Magnificent,' agreed Rebecca unhappily. 'But we must get back. As it is we will be late——'

'Oh, Rebecca!' He came to lean on her car door, his eyes lazily caressing. 'Are you always so concerned with what is right and what is wrong?'

Rebecca slid across the bench seat and climbed out at his side, escaping from his nearness. As usual he succeeded in disconcerting her.

With a sigh, he straightened, and then said: 'Come here. We'll sit down for a while. Do you smoke? I am afraid I have only cheroots.'

Rebecca shook her head. 'No, I don't smoke.' Her face was anxious.

Piers seated himself on a stretch of turf that was warmed by the heat of the sun and shaded by the outcrop of rock from which the waterfall tumbled. Taking out his cheroots, he lit one lazily, and drew deeply upon it. Then he looked up at her, shaking his head curiously.

'Tell me,' he said, 'what is causing that anxious frown?'

Rebecca turned away, breathing swiftly. Suddenly she was remembering something she had thought long forgotten, the reason she had left England in the first place. Her grandmother had been dead before she finished her training, of course, and she had shared a flat with another nurse. Sheila had been engaged to a young houseman, Peter Feldman, and naturally Peter became a frequent visitor at the flat. Unfortunately, after a time, Peter became attracted to Rebecca, and she to him. It had been an impossible situation. Sheila had been such a nice girl, a good friend, too good to be hurt like that. As soon as Rebecca qualified, she had jumped at the chance of this post, thousands of miles away from temptation. For a time she had thought she had loved Peter, but in these new and exciting surroundings she had found it easy to forget. In consequence, she had been grateful for the discovery that what she had felt for him had been no lasting emotion. Piers St. Clair presented entirely different problems. This man aroused her in a way she had not believed she could be aroused. Without touching her, without any visible effort on his part, he could reduce her to a trembling mass of emotions.

She was startled out of her thoughts when suddenly Piers spoke in her ear. She had been so absorbed that she had not been aware of his moving, but now he said: 'Why are you afraid of me, Rebecca?'

She opened her mouth to protest, but closed it again. It was true after all. She was afraid of him; or at least afraid of the power he could exert over her.

As she would have moved away, his fingers curved round her upper arm, and he sighed heavily. 'Dear

47

God, why did I have to meet you?' he murmured huskily.

Rebecca quivered in his grasp. 'We must go back,' she insisted weakly.

'Must we?' He regarded her intently, his eyes dark and yet disturbingly caressing. 'I don't want to go back. Do you?'

'Oh, Piers!' she said pleadingly. 'This—this is——'

'Crazy?' He shrugged, stroking her cheek with his free hand. 'But sometimes we have to do crazy things.' He bent his head and put his mouth against her arm, caressing it insistently. 'Such soft skin,' he murmured, against her flesh. 'Childlike. But you're not a child, are you, Rebecca? You're a woman, and you are wanting me just as much as I am wanting you.'

'*No!*' Rebecca pulled herself away from him. 'No, you're wrong!'

He didn't attempt to detain her and she looked back at him almost fearfully, a hand pressed to her mouth. He watched her for a long disturbing moment, and then he dragged his gaze away from her and stared out across the island to the sea in the distance. There was a moment when she wanted to go back to him, to slide her arms about him and press herself against the hard length of his body, but before it could manifest itself he moved, striding abruptly towards the car. '*Allons!*' he snapped commandingly, and with stumbling steps she hastened to join him.

The drive back to the villa was accomplished as silently as on the outward journey, and when they approached the entrance to Adele's drive Piers stood on his brakes, almost throwing Rebecca forward into the windscreen. Leaning past her, he thrust open her door and on trembling legs she climbed out. Without a word, he slammed the car into gear and drove away.

To her surprise, Adele was still resting when she returned. She was awake, and her bright, birdlike eyes turned expectantly, Rebecca thought, as she entered the bedroom. 'Well?' demanded the older woman impatiently. 'Where have you been, miss?'

Rebecca closed the door, smoothing her skirt. She had hastily donned her uniform, hoping that with it would come the assurance of her profession.

'I've been driving with Monsieur St. Clair,' she responded quietly. 'I'm sorry if I'm late. How do you feel? Did you have a good rest?'

'Now wait a minute!' Adele surveyed Rebecca's withdrawn features and the flickering evasion of her eyes, and her own expression became curious. 'What's the matter with you? Surely you realise you can't produce a statement like that without explaining yourself? How did you come to go driving with Piers?'

Rebecca sighed. 'He came while you were asleep. He invited me out for a while. I accepted. I'm sorry if you object——'

Adele plucked impatiently at the bedspread. 'Now wait a minute, wait a minute! I didn't say I objected did I?' She frowned, and leaned forward conspiratorially. 'What happened?'

Rebecca's colour deepened. 'What do you mean— what happened? What could happen? Nothing, of course.' She began to fold back the bed-covers, preparatory to getting Adele out of bed.

Adele looked disappointed. 'Did he say why he'd invited you out?' she asked persistently.

Rebecca sighed. 'I imagine he was at a loose end,' she remarked, as casually as she could. 'Is it important? He's not likely to ask me again.'

Adele stared at her. 'Why? What happened?'

Rebecca strove to keep her temper. She knew Adele was avid for any information she could get, but in this instance she could not satisfy her. She could not discuss what had occurred between herself and Piers St. Clair as though it were an experiment that had been carried out and the results were to be analysed. Besides, she didn't altogether care for this amount of interest to be

49

shown. There was something unhealthy about it and it was the first time Adele had ever sanctioned such a relationship. It was as though through her Adele was gaining a certain amount of vicarious enjoyment, and Rebecca wondered suddenly whether that was why Adele was so inquisitive. The idea was repugnant, and she tried to change the subject, but Adele would not be diverted.

'For heaven's sake, girl,' she exclaimed. 'Can't I show a bit of interest when my nurse attracts the attention of a man like Piers St. Clair?'

Rebecca helped Adele out of bed and began to fasten her garments. With deliberate emphasis, she said: 'I should imagine, from what you've told me, that any reasonably attractive female would attract the attention of Piers St. Clair.'

Adele looked up at her, her expression malicious. 'What's the matter, Rebecca?' she asked spitefully. 'Are you jealous?'

Rebecca stared back at her angrily. 'No, of course not——' she began indignantly, and then stopped, pressing her lips together. She would not allow Adele to arouse her. That was exactly what she wanted, and she refused to give her the satisfaction. Instead, she picked up the comb and began to do Adele's hair, smoothing the brittle, brassy strands into gentle waves.

Adele hunched her shoulders sulkily when it became obvious that Rebecca would not be drawn and found fault with everything Rebecca did for her. She refused to wear the shoes her nurse produced for her approval and demanded sandals instead. Without rancour, Rebecca smiled, and putting the offending articles away, fetched the sandals Adele wanted from her wardrobe. Then she wheeled Adele's chair through to the lounge where Rosa was already serving afternoon tea. Adele insisted upon pouring and deliberately spilt some of the hot liquid on to the soft rug at her feet. Rebecca was forced to fetch a cloth and wipe it up and she felt sure Adele would have liked to have spilled the burning liquid on her.

At last, when it became obvious that Rebecca was not to be aroused, Adele grew tired of the effort, and picked up a magazine. Rebecca excused herself and went to tidy the bedroom Adele had just left and her own room. She had little heart in the task, and losing patience with herself she sank down on to her bed staring blindly at her reflection in the dressing-table mirror.

If only she had never met Piers St. Clair, she thought despairingly. How much simpler life had been ten days ago. She had been content then, content with her life, even content with Adele's idiosyncrasies. But Piers had spoiled all that, aroused in her a realisation of what life could be like with a man like him. Was she a fool to reject what was offered even if there was no permanency in it? She knew little about him except that he was rich, that he had been married, and that his wife was dead. And Adele had told her all that. He had actually told her nothing about himself. Had he any family? And if he had—where were they? She sighed. He was an enigma, and enigmas were unfathomable, weren't they? ...

The next morning Rebecca encountered Piers St. Clair on the beach.

She had been down for her swim as usual, and was just walking, dripping, out of the water when he came down the beach towards her. Immediately Rebecca slid her arms into the sleeves of her towelling jacket, wrapping it almost protectively about her. Piers halted a couple of yards from her, taking out a case of cheroots and lighting one deliberately. The golden haze of dawn still hung about the sky, and the smoke from the small cigar curled upwards to join the faint mist above the palms.

Rebecca wrung out her hair, and endeavoured to smooth it behind her ears, but small curly tendrils insisted upon falling forward beside her cheeks. For a moment she considered walking away and leaving him, but suddenly he said:

'I came to apologise, Rebecca. For my actions yesterday. *Mon Dieu,* I am not usually so ill-mannered.'

Rebecca stared at him in surprise, wondering whether he was serious or merely using this as another attempt to amuse himself at her expense. But his dark face was perfectly serious and there was a rather remote detachment in his eyes.

She spread her hand expressively, lifting her shoulders in a helpless gesture of acceptance. 'It's all right,' she said inadequately. 'There's no harm done.'

'Isn't there?' Piers watched her broodingly. Then he raked a hand through his hair and turned away. 'How is your employer this morning? Or is she still asleep?'

Rebecca frowned. 'Adele sleeps until nine or thereabouts. I told you.'

He glanced at her, long lashes veiling his eyes. 'So you did.' He shrugged. 'I was merely making polite conversation, that is all.'

'Oh!' Rebecca bent her head. 'It's—it's a lovely morning, isn't it? What do you plan to do today?'

There was silence for a while and then he said: 'I have to meet the minister later this morning. This afternoon——' he shrugged. 'Who knows? I might take a trip to the islands. I only have another week here, and I ought to visit the tourist attractions.'

'Another week,' murmured Rebecca, looking up. 'And then—what?'

He drew deeply on his cheroot. 'Paris, I suppose,' he replied indifferently. 'I have a house there—just outside of the city.'

'You have only one home?' she enquired, with interest.

He gave a wry smile. 'Home? I have no —*home!*'

52

Rebecca's eyes widened. 'You're not serious, of course.'

'I am perfectly serious,' he returned harshly. 'I have four houses, however. That is really what you wanted to know, isn't it?'

Rebecca turned away. 'I'm not interested in your possessions, if that's what you're implying!' she exclaimed hotly.

He hesitated, and then sighed. 'Are you not? Then you are indeed unique, *mademoiselle*.'

Rebecca bent her head, studying the ovals of her nails with intensity. Why didn't she leave now? Go before anything more was said?

She felt, rather than heard, him move. He came round her with his panther-like stride, and regarded her bent head solemnly. 'Forgive me again,' he said, rather bleakly. 'I seem adept at saying and doing the wrong things where you are concerned.'

'It's not important,' Rebecca said, twisting the belt of her jacket tortuously.

'Obviously not, to you!' observed Piers rather harshly. 'And of course, it never occurred to you that our frequent meetings are anything more than coincidence!'

Rebecca looked up at him with startled eyes. 'I don't know what you mean,' she said awkwardly. 'I think I'd better go——'

Piers uttered an ejaculation in his own language, raking a careless hand through his hair. 'Yes, yes!' he snapped coldly. 'Go! That is what you always do when the situation becomes too difficult to handle, isn't it?'

Rebecca bit her lower lip hard. 'I just don't see any point in this conversation,' she began.

'Do you not?' He ran a hand round the back of his neck, flexing his muscles. 'Or is it not perhaps true that you are afraid to continue with it?'

Rebecca hesitated, and then she sighed. 'All right,

53

all right,' she said tautly. 'I have realised that I have been singled out for attention by the powerful Piers St. Clair. I'm flattered.' Then as his expression hardened, she went on: 'But I just don't see any point in discussing it. What do you want from me? I'm not one of your society women. I'm not versed in the intricacies of selling myself to the highest bidder, and nor do I want to be!'

'*Tu chienne!*' Piers had paled a little under his tan. 'How dare you speak to me like that?'

In truth, Rebecca didn't know that either. Her words had seemed to run away with her and now she felt ashamed. 'I'm—I'm sorry,' she said at last. 'I—I don't know what came over me.'

Piers ground out his cheroot with his heel in the sand. 'It is obvious we have both been mistaken in our judgements,' he said in controlled tones. 'I will bid you *au revoir, mademoiselle.*'

He turned abruptly and walked away along the beach and Rebecca stood looking after him unhappily. Her whole being longed to run after him and beg him to forgive her. She wanted to tell him that everything she had said had been the result of tortured emotions stretched to breaking point, but how could she? And if she did no doubt he would laugh at her. After all, his reasons for wanting her were vastly different from her reasons for wanting him.

Taking a deep breath, she began to trudge miserably up the beach. She felt certain now that she would never see him again and the realisation was terrifying. She was so absorbed with her thoughts that she did not see the sand crab in her path until she stood on it and sharp pincers punctured her foot before the creature scuttled away sideways to the safety of the water.

Letting out a cry of dismay, she sank down on to the sand, gripping her injured foot tightly, and bent to examine the damage. Blood oozed from the lacerations and as she tentatively allowed her foot to rest on the sand it mingled with it. The incident seemed the last straw so far as Rebecca was concerned. Her injuries were only slight, but allied to her depression they were sufficient to reduce her to tears.

With an aching sob, she lay back on the sand and allowed the scalding tears to run unheeded down her cheeks.

Her arm shading her eyes, she did not immediately notice the shadow that came to lie across her, and only when she sensed someone's scrutiny did she look up. Then she sat up abruptly, rubbing vigorously at her cheeks to banish the betraying marks.

Piers looked down at her with distant eyes, and said: 'What is wrong? What have you done? I heard you cry out.'

Rebecca shook her head. 'It's nothing,' she denied, sniffing.

Piers' eyes surveyed the length of her body with disturbing intensity, and then came to rest on the blood-stained sand beside her foot. With an exclamation, he went down on his haunches and lifted her foot experimentally. Rebecca suffered his examination, and when he looked up, said: 'I told you. It's nothing. I stood on a crab, that's all.'

'You must put some antiseptic salve on it when you get back to the villa,' he said, smoothing the sand from her skin. Then he bent his head and sucked hard at each of the punctures, spitting the blood and sand away. Rebecca watched him, resting back on her elbows, her brows drawn together incredulously. When he had finished, he said: 'Don't you know that that is the most effective way to prevent poison from entering the body?' He shrugged, wiping his mouth with the back of his hand. 'Primitive, perhaps, to someone with your nursing experience, but effective nevertheless.'

'Thank you.' Rebecca pressed her lips together.

Piers allowed her foot to drop back on to the sand, but he did not get up. Instead, he sat regarding her with a strange expression on his lean dark face. 'Why were you crying?' he asked softly.

Rebecca shook her head helplessly. 'It was stupid. The—the injury was nothing——'

'I don't believe that was why you were crying,' he said, his voice harsh. 'Can't you even be honest with yourself, Rebecca?' He moved suddenly, and swung her up into his arms, standing upright. 'I'll take you back to the villa. It is well not to risk getting poison into your foot.'

Rebecca protested, but he ignored her, and she gave in at last and allowed herself to enjoy the sensation of being this close to him for a while at least. He did not look at her as he strode easily across the turf and into the house, but she was aware of him with every fibre of her being. The hardness of his arms, of the muscular width of his chest, was sensuously disturbing, and she could feel the heat of his body and smell the clean male smell about him.

'Where is your room?' he enquired in low tones as he stood in the centre of the hall, and Rebecca spread a hand expressively.

'If you'll put me down, I can manage myself,' she said, quietly, half fearful that either Adele or Rosa might hear them.

His eyes bored into hers. 'Are you going to tell me, or do I find out by a process of elimination?' he asked, with cool mockery.

Rebecca sighed and pointed down the corridor. Piers nodded and strode down the passage and when they reached her door she indicated it. It stood slightly ajar, and he pushed it open and walked in. The bed stood unmade, the covers tumbled, while her clothes were strewn around. Piers walked over to the bed and bent to deposit her upon it, and Rebecca put her hands round his neck to steady herself. His skin was smooth to the touch and her fingers lingered so that when he would have straightened she prevented him.

'Let me go, Rebecca,' he muttered in a tortured voice, reaching up to wrench her arms from around his neck, but she would not unlink her fingers and with a groan he sank down beside her. His eyes were dark and tormented as he stared down at her, his hands encircling her throat, and then with a muffled exclamation he bent his head and parted her mouth with his.

Rebecca had been kissed before, but never like this. Never so hungrily, so urgently, that his touch destroyed any inhibitions she might have felt. One hand slid over her shoulder and down her arm to her waist, loosening the beach jacket and probing her soft flesh so that all coherent thought was impossible. He was no amateur, she realised, when it came to lovemaking, but what disturbed her most was the realisation that she could be as demanding as he, responding to his undoubted expertise with abandonment. The weight of his hard body on hers had a seducing quality about it, and when suddenly he dragged himself away from her she felt bereft.

He turned away, raking a hand through his hair, shaking his head with slow emphasis. '*Non!*' he muttered thickly. '*Non!* I must not do it!'

Rebecca stared at his back, a frown marring her flushed features, and presently he turned and looked at her with impassioned eyes. 'Rebecca,' he said huskily, 'I must go!'

Rebecca propped herself up on one elbow, the attitude unknowingly provocative. 'Are you running away, Piers?' she murmured softly.

He hunched his shoulders, thrusting his hands deep into his trousers' pockets. 'Yes! Yes, I am,' he said, his eyes surveying her with devastating intensity. 'I find even I cannot destroy such innocence!' His expression hardened.

Rebecca's frown deepened and she slid off the bed. 'Piers,' she murmured questioningly, 'I—I know what I am doing.'

He raised his eyes heavenward. 'I doubt it, Rebecca,' he muttered grimly. 'Please, don't make it any harder for me than it already is. For the first time in my life, after years with a woman I loathe and despise, I have found something beautiful—something worthwhile! But—God help me! I cannot take it.' He turned away abruptly. 'I must go. Adele will be awake soon, and if she finds me here——'

Rebecca caught his arm. 'Piers?' she murmured, shaking her head. 'What are you talking about? I—I haven't asked you for anything—I don't expect any-thing——'

He caught her shoulders and shook her gently. 'Haven't you been listening to me?' he asked fiercely. 'Look, we can't discuss this now. There isn't time, and in any case I need time to—to——' He shook his head again. 'Tonight—*oui*? Meet me tonight. We can talk then.'

Rebecca stared at him. 'All right. But how? I mean —Adele——'

'I'll come here. To the beach. About nine, right?'

Rebecca swallowed hard. 'All right.'

'Good.' He gave her a faint smile, and then with an exclamation he caught her close for a moment and pressed his mouth to hers. '*Tu es adorable! Je t'aime!*' he murmured huskily, and then without allowing her to say another word, he went swiftly out of the door.

After he had gone, Rebecca moved on trembling legs to close the door, and once that was accomplished she leaned back against it weakly. The events of the past few minutes had been infinitely too momentous for her to be able to assimilate them with any degree of coherency. What did it all mean? What did *Piers* mean? Those final few words in his own language; could he possibly have been serious? He had said she was adorable—that he *loved* her! Was it possible? Could he love her? And if he did, what did he intend to do about it?

She moved like an automaton to the dressing table, forcing herself to concentrate on the face of her alarm clock. It was almost eight-thirty. It was time she was dressed and having breakfast. Rosa would begin to get curious if she was late.

Shaking her head, trying to bring normality back into her life, she went into the bathroom and under a cold shower put all thoughts of Piers St. Clair to the back of her mind. The hours between now and nine o'clock tonight stretched endlessly away ahead of her, and the only way to make them pass was to fill her day to the exclusion of all conscious thought . . .

CHAPTER FOUR

Rosa was not in the kitchen when Rebecca made her appearance, and she looked about her, puzzled. The housekeeper was always there at this time of the morning, preparing Adele's tray, and evidences of her recent occupation were all about, so she must be somewhere. Rebecca decided she must have gone outside to gather some vegetables for lunch, and shrugging, she poured herself a cup of coffee from the pot on the electric cooker. She was seated at the kitchen table, drinking it, when Rosa came in from the hall.

'Good morning, Rosa.' Rebecca smiled.

'Good morning, miss.' Rosa did not smile, but made her way to the sink unit. 'Did you get some coffee?'

'Yes, thanks. You weren't here, so I helped myself.' She frowned, noticing Rosa's preoccupation. 'Is—is something wrong?'

Rosa glanced round, her normally amiable face slightly anxious. 'Not really, miss. I—I've been taking in Miss Adele's tray.'

Rebecca's coffee cup clattered into its saucer. 'You've been what?'

'Taking in Miss Adele's tray,' repeated Rosa stolidly. 'She asked for it, miss. I had to.'

Rebecca shook her head uncomprehendingly. 'She *asked* for it?'

'Yes, miss. At first I thought you were about, too. Miss Adele came to the kitchen, in her chair.'

Rebecca got rather jerkily to her feet. 'She came to the kitchen in her chair!' she repeated incredulously. 'I'm sorry if I sound stupid, Rosa, but this has never happened before. Not since I've been here anyway.'

'I know, miss. I was surprised, too.' Rosa's round face

showed her concern. 'I guess she woke early or something.'

Rebecca was thinking hard. All of a sudden a lot of things were occurring to her. 'How—how long ago was this?' she asked. 'When Miss Adele came to the kitchen, I mean.'

Rosa considered. 'Fifteen or twenty minutes, I suppose,' she said thoughtfully.

Fifteen or twenty minutes! Rebecca closed her eyes for a long moment. When she opened them again, Rosa was eyeing her with concern. Sensing the elderly servant's anxiety, Rebecca managed a faint smile. 'It's all right, Rosa,' she reassured her. 'I was just—thinking, that's all.' She bit hard at her upper lip. 'Did—did Miss Adele say anything when you took in her tray?'

'No, miss. Just to tell you that she had been up and about.'

Rebecca walked restlessly across to the window, and back again. It was hard trying to find reasons for anything Adele did, and even now she might be jumping to conclusions unnecessarily. But somehow she was certain she was not. She took a deep breath. Whatever the situation, Adele had to be faced, and after all, there was no harm done, was there? Adele had practically encouraged her to go out with Piers St. Clair. Surely she could not object because he had brought her back from the beach.

But was there more to it than that? Had Adele seen them or heard them together in the hall? Or had she followed them to Rebecca's bedroom? Rebecca's face suffused with hot colour. Oh, no! Surely Adele would not have done that! She tried to remember whether her door had been open or closed. It had been open, of course. Piers had pushed it open when he brought her home and afterwards ... She shook her head. They would not have noticed if an onlooker had come silently to that aperture and sat for a while watching them.

An awful feeling of nausea overwhelmed her, and she turned away so that Rosa should not see the pallor of her face. She must not jump to conclusions like this! Just because Adele had been up and about did not mean she had seen or heard anything. Even so ...

She walked to the door. 'I'll go and see if she has finished yet,' she said, in a taut voice, and went out of the kitchen.

In the corridor she halted again. Why was she torturing herself like this? What did it matter if Adele had seen them? Nothing had happened—nothing of which to be ashamed, at least.

Straightening her shoulders, she marched down the hall to Adele's room, and after knocking, she entered. Adele was sitting up in her wheelchair, the breakfast tray across her knees. She was not dressed, but she had put on her dressing gown. She gave Rebecca a curiously triumphant look as she came into the room, and Rebecca swallowed hard before saying: 'Good morning, Miss St. Cloud,' in a deliberately casual tone.

Adele put aside the tray, thrusting it on to a small table beside her, and wiping her mouth on her napkin. 'Good morning, Rebecca,' she answered amiably. 'Lovely morning, isn't it?'

Rebecca compressed her lips. That was an unusual greeting. Adele invariably woke up in a foul mood and had to be humoured at this hour. But taking her cue, she replied: 'It is indeed. Beautiful.' She managed a bright smile. The room was filled with sunlight, and her gaze flickered to the venetian blinds at the windows which someone had opened to their fullest extent. 'You're up particularly early this morning.'

'Yes.' Adele lay back in her chair with obvious enjoyment. 'Perhaps the brightness of the day disturbed me—or could it have been something else, do you suppose?'

Rebecca managed to retain her composure. 'Did you draw the venetian blinds?' she asked, crossing to adjust them so that the brilliance of the sunlight did not dazzle her patient.

Adele nodded. 'Yes, I did. Take a look out there, Rebecca. Have you ever realised what a magnificent view I have?'

Rebecca looked out. Adele's windows were further along the same wall of the house as the hall windows, overlooking the sweep of grass that led down to the beach. Anyone sitting at this window would have a magnificent view of everything and everybody that moved out there.

Rebecca swung round. 'It—it is—magnificent!' she agreed.

Adele nodded. 'I often sit by that window, Rebecca. Not always in the mornings, I must admit, but sometimes. This morning I was restless, so I sat there for a while.'

Rebecca felt the muscles of her face freeze. 'Oh, yes,' she managed stiffly.

'Yes. I saw you go down for your swim, Rebecca. How I envy you——'

'Stop it!' Rebecca could stand no more. 'What are you trying to say, Miss St. Cloud? You are trying to say something, aren't you?'

Adele stared at her in apparent surprise. 'Dear me, Rebecca, you are touchy this morning. Whatever do you imagine I am trying to say?'

Rebecca took a deep breath. 'Have you finished with your breakfast tray, Miss St. Cloud? If you have I'll take it back to the kitchen.'

Adele's expression hardened slightly. 'All in good time, miss, all in good time. Come and sit down. I want you to tell me all about yesterday afternoon.'

'Yesterday afternoon?' Rebecca stared at her in astonishment. 'What happened yesterday afternoon?'

Adele raised her eyebrows. 'Your trip with Piers. I want to hear all about it.'

Rebecca moved restlessly. 'There's nothing to hear.

Please, Miss St. Cloud, let me take the tray and then you can have your bath.'

Adele plucked at the cord of her dressing gown. 'Later, Rebecca, later. Right now we have other matters to discuss. I—er—well, I think I ought to tell you a little about Piers.'

Rebecca felt sick. 'I—I don't want to talk about Monsieur St. Clair,' she stated firmly.

Adele's eyes narrowed. 'Nevertheless, we will talk about him, Rebecca. If only for your own good.'

Rebecca stared at her now. 'What is that supposed to mean?'

Adele shrugged. 'Well, my dear, I venture to say I know him a little better than you do, and I just wonder whether I have been foolish in allowing you to—well, associate with him.'

Rebecca raised her eyes heavenward. 'You didn't allow me to do anything,' she exclaimed impatiently. 'I—I'm perfectly capable of making my own decisions, thank you.'

Adele sighed. 'I wonder. I wonder. Poor Jennifer thought so, too, and look where it's landed her!' She shook her head regretfully.

Rebecca pressed her lips together. She would not be inquisitive. She must not be inquisitive. That was exactly what Adele wanted. Even so . . .

Adele watched the expressive features of her face, and went on: 'Poor Jennifer. I did tell you about her, didn't I? My sister, you know.'

Rebecca heaved a sigh. 'The one who married Piers, I assume.'

'Yes, that's right. My sister Jennifer. It's almost eight years since I've seen her.'

Rebecca was piling plates and saucers together on the tray, preparatory to picking it up, but something Adele said made her look at her with suddenly curious eyes. 'But she's dead!' she said, almost involuntarily.

Adele's eyes widened and she looked at Rebecca

almost indignantly. 'Jennifer? Dead? When did it happen?'

Rebecca gave an exasperated gesture. 'You told me so yourself,' she exclaimed impatiently.

'Oh, no! No, I didn't do that.'

Rebecca felt as though a cold hand was sliding into her stomach and slowly and systematically squeezing it. 'But you did!' she contradicted Adele urgently. 'Don't you remember? We were talking about Piers and—and the fact of his being married—and you said your sister was dead!'

'Oh, I see.' Adele nodded. 'My dear Rebecca, you've got confused! I did say my sister was dead, I remember now. But not Piers' wife; not Jennifer! *Denise!*'

Rebecca felt nausea welling up inside her. Piers was married! *He was married!* She couldn't take it in. She couldn't accept it. It was bad enough before, knowing of the enormous gulf between them, but this—this was terrible; agonising; destructive!

She stared tortuously at Adele and suddenly as she looked at her she realised something. Adele had planned this! She had deliberately misled her about Piers' marriage, knowing that when Rebecca eventually found out it would be so much more painful. Maybe she had planned to wait until what had happened this morning had happened. Which brought her back to this morning, and the reason for Adele's early explorations.

Uncaring of the consequences, Rebecca exclaimed: 'You saw us this morning, didn't you?'

Adele feigned surprise. 'Saw who, Rebecca?'

Rebecca clenched her fists. 'Oh, you know, *you know*!' she cried angrily. 'You saw me with Piers! But when? And where?' She raised a hand to her forehead. 'You couldn't—you couldn't have——' She turned away, suddenly, unable to go on.

Adele uttered an ugly sound of amusement. 'Couldn't what, Rebecca? Couldn't what?' She propelled her chair round the trembling girl. 'I'll tell you, shall I? You think I couldn't have wheeled this old chair along the corridor to your bedroom—yes, your bedroom, miss—and watched Piers making love to you!' She snorted contemptuously. 'Well, you're wrong, miss. I could! And what's more, I did!'

'No!' Rebecca pressed the palm of her hand to her mouth.

'Oh, yes, miss.' Adele's face was contorted with triumph. 'Yes, I watched you, and it's given me a new lease on life, believe me!'

Rebecca stared at her, repelled and yet fascinated. 'I don't begin to understand your motives. You're twisted! *Evil!*'

'Maybe I am.' Adele was without remorse. 'But I don't care.'

Rebecca shook her head helplessly. 'But what have you gained by it? A chance to hurt me, is that it?'

Adele's lip curled. 'That's a small thing compared to knowing that the man who deserted me for Jennifer is no more reliable now than he was then!'

Rebecca froze. 'Piers? What do you mean—deserted you?'

Adele sneered, 'I told you before, Rebecca. When Piers first came here. We were once going to be married.' She stared broodingly into space. 'He wanted me, I know he did. But Jennifer wouldn't leave him alone. And he thought she was perfect. As perfect as her appearance!' Adele laughed cruelly. 'Oh, but he was wrong, and he soon found out!' She looked hard at Rebecca. 'He married her, Rebecca, because she was pregnant! What else could he do?'

Rebecca shook her head, unable to accept what the other woman was saying. It was ghastly, like a nightmare!

Adele heaved a sigh. 'So now you know the whole story. Pitiful, isn't it? I was only a girl then, and Jennifer only a little older.'

But Rebecca could feel no pity now for this shrivel-led-up shell of a woman who was prepared to use her own nurse in an attempt to gain a vicarious revenge on her own sister—and on Piers. She was sickened, repelled by her viciousness, unable to stay in the same room as Adele St. Cloud. Grasping the tray, she made her way to the door, and somehow got outside. Stumbling a little, she made her way to the kitchen, thrusting the tray on to the kitchen table and collapsing weakly into a chair. The awful pallor of her face attracted Rosa's concern, and she came round to her anxiously.

'Miss! Miss!' she cried. 'What is it? What's wrong? Are you ill?'

Rebecca shook her head dazedly, and then looked up into Rosa's kind, normal face. 'Just tell me something, Rosa,' she murmured huskily. 'Is—is Monsieur St. Clair married, do you know?'

Rosa stared at her frowningly, and then looked knowingly towards the kitchen door. 'Monsieur St. Clair?' she echoed. 'I—I don't know, miss. I never met him before he came here a couple of weeks ago.'

Rebecca nodded resignedly. 'I—I see.' She swallowed hard. 'Do—do you have any more coffee, Rosa? I could surely do with some.'

Rosa moved quickly. 'Of course I have,' she exclaimed. 'Just a minute!'

Over several cups of strong black coffee Rebecca tried to make sense of everything that had happened. But it was difficult in her confused state and time and again she had to tell herself that it was not just some crazy dream. But Adele's maliciousness was real enough, and so was the aching pain in the pit of her stomach when she considered the outcome of her abortive relationship with Piers St. Clair.

Was this why he had controlled himself this morning? Was this why he had called her innocent? Did he know that she was uninformed of his marital arrangements? Or did he think she was the kind of girl to indulge in an adulterous affair with him? The implications were legion. What must he think of her? If Adele had purposely avoided telling her that he was married, she was almost bound to have told Piers that Rebecca did know. After all, she couldn't risk his telling her and thus ruining the potentialities of their involvement with one another. And what did she think she had seen this morning? What imagined construction had she put upon those moments when she was in Piers' arms? Did she believe that their lovemaking had exceeded the bounds of what was right and what was wrong? And did it matter what she thought, when she could so easily make her own explanations so convincing?

Rebecca buried her face in her hands, and Rosa came to the table and touched her arm gently. 'What is it?' she asked softly. 'Can I help?'

Rebecca managed a faint wistful smile, but she shook her head. 'No one can help, Rosa,' she said quietly. Smoothing the flesh over her cheekbones, she rose determinedly to her feet. 'I'm going out, Rosa,' she said with dignity. 'You can tell Miss St. Cloud that I will return later for my things.'

Rosa was aghast. 'You're leaving, miss?'

'Yes, I am.' Rebecca bit her lip. 'Something has happened, something that makes it impossible for me to stay.'

Rosa shook her head, folding her arms across her ample bosom. 'Are you sure you know what you're doing, miss?' she asked worriedly. 'You look mighty queer to me. Oughtn't you to wait a while, a couple of days maybe, until you have time to think?'

Rebecca shook her head again. 'I—I couldn't stay in this house,' she averred swiftly. 'Excuse me, now. I must go and change.'

Before changing, however, Rebecca rang Dr. Manson and told him of her decision. Naturally he was shocked at her decision, particularly as she would give him no reason for this abrupt departure. He said she was placing him in an intolerable position, but Rebecca knew that it would be an easy matter for him to send a nurse out from his clinic for a few days until Adele was able to obtain a replacement.

Then she rang for a taxi, and while she waited for its appearance she changed into a slim-fitting shift of ice blue cotton and secured her hair in a pleat at the back of her head.

Once she was ready, she was impatient for the taxi to arrive, for she had packed an overnight case and she had no desire to have to explain her actions to Adele. But presently the cab purred smoothly up the drive and she ran out and climbed in without speaking to anyone. She gave the address of a hotel in Suva and then sank back against the soft upholstery. She was not surprised to find she was crying and taking a tissue from her handbag she dabbed impatiently at her eyes. This was no time for tears. What she had to do must be done before she lost the courage to do it.

The Hotel Avenida was in a quiet street off the main thoroughfares of the city, and Rebecca had passed it often on her trips here. She was able to book a single room for one night, and then called the airport and made enquiries about reservations to London.

Over a sandwich in the hotel restaurant, she considered how she was going to get in touch with Piers. She had no idea which hotel he was staying at, and there were dozens in Suva itself. Apart from anything else, it was unlikely that any hotel receptionist would tell her if he was staying there. Men like Piers St. Clair were not troubled by unnecessary phone calls, and no one would believe she knew him and did not even know where he was staying.

Finally she came up with a solution. He had said he was meeting the minister this morning. Might she possibly catch him there? It was only twelve-thirty. He could conceivably be lunching with the minister.

She searched the phone book in the hotel lobby for the number, and then, with controlled tones, asked for Monsieur St. Clair. The receptionist at the ministry was very polite, and explained that Monsieur St. Clair had left several minutes earlier. Perhaps the caller would be able to contact him at his hotel. Rebecca searched her mind wildly for some excuse not to know the hotel, and the receptionist said: 'Excuse me, madam, I have a call on the other line.'

With a sinking heart, Rebecca banged down the receiver. So much for her bright ideas. Now what was she to do?

She walked dejectedly across the hotel lobby, and the young receptionist eyed her curiously. 'Is something wrong, Miss Lindsay?' he enquired politely.

Rebecca smiled faintly. 'Not really, thank you.'

'I could not help but overhear you asking for a guest of the minister's,' said the young man deferentially. 'Have you tried the Suva Nova Hotel? The minister's guests invariably stay there.'

Rebecca's eyes widened. 'Oh!' she said, swallowing hard. 'Oh, do they? Well, thank—thank you!'

Turning back to the kiosk, she flicked through the book again and found the number of the Suva Nova Hotel. When the receptionist there answered, she said: 'Could I speak to Monsieur St. Clair, please?'

'I am sorry. Monsieur St. Clair is lunching with some friends today,' replied the receptionist regretfully. 'Can I give him a message as soon as he comes in?'

Rebecca hesitated. At least she now knew where he was staying. 'No—no, that won't be necessary,' she declined quickly.

'Who shall I say was calling?' enquired the receptionist persistently.

Rebecca panicked a little. 'It's of no importance,' she replied, and replaced her receiver.

When she walked back across the hall, she handed the receptionist a coin. 'Thanks,' she said, with a faint smile. 'I'm very grateful.'

'We try to be of assistance,' answered the clerk smilingly. 'And—thank you, Miss Lindsay.'

Rebecca left the hotel at about two o'clock in the afternoon. A somnolent heat haze hung over everything, and the streets were markedly quieter. Few people shunned the rest period at this time of the day, but Rebecca could not rest, and she decided to walk to the Suva Nova Hotel.

The Suva Nova was an enormous place, the kind of international hostelry found in most large cities to cater for the businessman who demanded excellent service allied to an efficient communications system. Shallow marble steps led up to a series of swing glass doors, and after a moment's hesitation Rebecca mounted the steps and went inside.

The air-conditioned reception lounge stretched ahead of her, cool and mosaic-tiled, an abundance of flowering plants and shrubs on a network of trellises providing colour and fragrance. Polished leather chairs and couches looked cool and comfortable, and the only sounds were those that emanated from outside the building. Rebecca crossed the hall determinedly, conscious of the disturbing click of her heels on the tiles, but no one took any notice of her until she attracted the attention of one of two receptionists. The dark-skinned young man in his immaculate bronze suit regarded her distantly, and said:

'Yes, madam? Can I help you?'

Rebecca gripped her handbag tightly. 'Yes, yes, you can. I rang earlier, enquiring about Monsieur St. Clair. I was told he was out for lunch. Has he come in yet?'

The receptionist frowned. 'And your name, madam? If you'll give me your name, I'll see if he's in.'

Rebecca pressed her lips together for a moment, and

71

then sighed. 'It's Lindsay—*Miss* Lindsay.'

'Very well, Miss Lindsay. If you'll just take a seat I'll see if Monsieur St. Clair is available.'

Rebecca gave a resigned shrug of her shoulders and went and sat down. It was obvious Piers was in, otherwise she would have been told he was out by now. A few moments later the young man came across to her.

'Monsieur St. Clair will see you now, Miss Lindsay. If—you'll just follow me?'

Rebecca got to her feet. 'Oh, but—isn't he coming down?' she asked awkwardly.

The young man frowned. 'Monsieur St. Clair will see you in his suite, of course.'

'Of—of course.' Rebecca nodded. She should have guessed. Men like Piers St. Clair did not have hotel rooms; they had *suites*.

She followed the receptionist across to one of the many lifts and they rode upwards for a considerable number of floors, emerging on to a corridor carpeted in dark grey pile. The young man escorted her to a white door whose number was picked out in gold letters and then bowed himself away. Rebecca looked after him, and then, with determination, knocked.

Almost at once the door was opened by Piers himself. He was wearing a dark lounge suit and looked superbly attractive, his linen contrasting sharply with the tan of his skin. He had obviously just come in and was in the process of loosening his tie and unbuttoning his shirt.

He looked at Rebecca with curious eyes, and stepping back indicated that she should enter. Rebecca did so, not without some misgivings. Confronting Piers St. Clair in his suite was rather like confronting the tiger in his lair. When the door was closed behind her and Rebecca was taking in some of the beauty of the blue and silver appointments of this most luxurious of lounges Piers came round her to regard her intently.

Rebecca coloured under his gaze, aware that several tendrils of hair had loosened themselves from her pleat and strayed about her neck, while the cotton dress was a little limp with the heat. Compared to his cool assurance she felt hot and untidy and very much aware of her own limitations.

'I—I'm sorry to come here like this,' she began tightly, 'but—but as I'm leaving Fiji tomorrow I thought——'

Piers stared at her with narrowed eyes. 'You're leaving Fiji?' he snapped, interrupting her abruptly.

Rebecca swallowed hard. 'That's right, and in—in spite of everything——'

'A moment, Rebecca.' Piers ran a hand round the back of his neck. 'Suppose you start at the beginning. Exactly why are you leaving Fiji?' His eyes suddenly darkened and he snapped his fingers. '*Naturellement*, I have it! Adele saw us this morning, am I not right?'

Rebecca's colour deepened. 'Yes—she saw us,' she agreed tonelessly.

Piers frowned. 'And she has—how do you say it?—fired you?'

'No.' Rebecca clenched her fists. 'No, I am leaving of my own accord.'

He stared at her uncomprehendingly. '*Mon Dieu*, Rebecca, what has happened, then?'

'Enough.' Rebecca trembled a little at the remembrance of it all. 'Piers, I want to know—are you married?'

His expression changed. 'You know I am,' he replied bitterly.

Rebecca's legs went weak, and she swayed a little. So it was true. Adele had not been lying. She stared at him despairingly. How could he stand there and admit it so indifferently?

Piers watched the colour drain out of her face, and with an ejaculation he cupped a hand round her neck and pulled her close to him, finding her mouth with

73

his own. The demanding pressure of that kiss robbed Rebecca of the will to resist and for a moment she responded, but then as the hardness of his body penetrated her consciousness she dragged herself away from him. Rubbing her mouth with her hand, she shook her head wildly. 'No,' she choked, *no*! Don't you understand? I didn't know. I never dreamed you were married. I thought your wife was dead.'

Piers' expression was grim. 'What do you mean, you didn't know?' he snapped harshly. 'Of course you knew. Adele told you the whole story.'

Rebecca continued to shake her head. 'Is that what she told you?' She gave a mirthless, brittle laugh. 'How clever she's been! Playing each of us off against the other!'

'What the hell are you talking about?' Piers grasped her shoulders in a cruel grip. 'Rebecca, look at me! What is this all about?'

Rebecca stared at him, gulping chokily. 'I've told you. I didn't know you were married!'

Piers' eyes narrowed. 'And this means much to you?'

Rebecca looked incredulously at him. 'Means much to me? Of course it means much to me! Piers, whatever you may think, I am not the kind of girl to—to get involved with another woman's husband!'

Piers shook her impatiently. 'Rebecca, listen to me! My marriage means nothing to me—don't you understand?'

Rebecca's eyes were tortured. 'How can you say that?' she exclaimed wonderingly. 'How can you say that to me!' She choked back a sob. 'This—this morning—Adele saw us, as you said. I don't know what she thinks she saw, but she took great pleasure in telling me afterwards everything she thought I should know about you!'

Piers heaved a sigh and released her. 'I see.'

'No, you don't see.' Rebecca chewed her lower lip.

'You don't seem to understand exactly what she did say!'

Piers gave an eloquent shrug of his shoulders. 'I know Adele well enough to know that anything she might say about me would not be complimentary.' He shook his head wearily. 'If you have come here to hear me deny what my dear sister-in-law said about me, then I am afraid you are to be disappointed.'

Rebecca shivered. 'Don't you care what she said?'

His eyes darkened slightly as he surveyed her slender form. '*Non*,' he answered huskily. 'All I care about is what you are going to say.'

Rebecca gave a helpless gesture. 'What can I say?' She bent her head. 'Oh, Piers, why did you have to be married?'

He allowed his hand to slide caressingly along her wrist, his thumb moving rhythmically against its inner vulnerability. 'I have asked myself that a dozen times —since I met you,' he said, rather thickly. 'Rebecca, I meant what I said this morning——'

'No!' Rebecca wrenched her hand away from him. 'No.'

Piers' eyes surveyed her penetratingly, their depths dark and enigmatic. 'No—what?'

Rebecca spread her hands. 'You're married, Piers. Anything that might have been between us—is over.'

'You don't believe that.' His tone was grim, but matter-of-fact.

'I've got to believe it.' Rebecca turned away, clenching her fists. 'You—you've never divorced . . .'

'*Non!*' Piers uttered a curse. 'Rebecca, we are Catholics. There has never been a divorce in my family!'

Rebecca's nails bit into the palms of her hands. 'I see.'

Piers' hand grasped the back of her neck suddenly, his fingers unloosening the pleat of hair so that it tumbled over his hand in a silky mass. Bending his head, he touched the back of her neck with his mouth and she quivered violently. '*Non*,' he groaned against her flesh, '*non*, you do not see, Rebecca. Let me tell you about my wife—about Jennifer——'

Rebecca closed her eyes in agony, willing herself not to lean back against him and allow him to continue making this gentle love to her. She moved away compulsively at last, and said: 'Adele told me about—Jennifer.'

Piers' face grew remote. 'And what did she say, I wonder? You would rather believe her than me, is that it?'

Rebecca spread her hands helplessly. 'What can there be said? You're married. I just wish you had never come to Fiji!'

Piers' face tautened as though she had struck him and he walked past her to the window, standing there with his back to her. Rebecca shook her head miserably. Why was it that she, the innocent party to all this, should feel guilty?

Finally he turned and said in a cold, expressionless voice: 'You say you're leaving?'

'Yes,' Rebecca nodded.

'Where will you go? To England?'

'Of course.'

'Of course,' he echoed bleakly. 'You will take another nursing post?'

Rebecca lifted her shoulders. 'In a hospital, if I can.'

He inclined his head. They might have become two strangers standing talking, exchanging trivialities. 'I suppose I should wish you luck,' he said. 'Will you see—Adele again?'

'No!' Rebecca spoke quickly. 'No. I shall telephone Rosa. She will pack my things and send them to me.'

'Tell me,' he asked savagely, 'do you always run away from your problems?'

Rebecca trembled visibly. What could she say? How could she answer such an accusation? For after all it was true. She had run away before—from Peter Feldman.

'I must go,' she said, turning to the door.

'Yes—go!' Piers eyes were cold and contemptuous. 'Get out of here!'

Rebecca wrenched open the door and somehow she got outside on to that beautiful pile-carpeted corridor. As she walked to the lift it was as though she was dazed and even when she emerged into the sunshine of the street there was no sense of reality about it. The reality was there—in that hotel suite—with Piers. But how could she go back and accept whatever it was he had intended to offer her? If nothing else she had always considered she had self-respect. But oh, how cold those words would sound in twenty years, she thought despairingly ...

PART TWO

CHAPTER ONE

REBECCA crossed the forecourt of St. Bartholomew's Hospital and entered the wide reception lounge. St. Bartholomew's was a new hospital and its lines were sleek and clean and modern, blending in well with the new estate that had been built round it. It was just outside of London in one of the new developments that was taking some of the overflow from the city's crowded suburbs.

Rebecca greeted the porters who were on duty in the hall and made her way up to her office adjoining Ward 15. Sister Annette Fleming, whom she had come to relieve, smiled at her as she came into the room and hung her cloak away in the closet.

'All quiet on the western front,' she observed, lightly. 'Gosh, am I glad you're here. I'm tired!'

Rebecca's eyes twinkled at her. 'You should go to bed when you're supposed to, instead of spending half your day with Barry Morrison. Doesn't he know night sisters need their sleep?'

Annette pushed back her chair. 'I find it difficult enough to sleep in daytime without the phone constantly ringing,' she exclaimed. She yawned, and pressed her hand to her mouth apologetically. 'You know what he's like.'

'Persistent!' remarked Rebecca dryly, picking up the record sheet Annette had been working upon. 'You'll have to tell him to be more patient. As a houseman himself, he ought to know better.'

Annette draped her cloak over her shoulders. 'There's some coffee in the pot if you want it. Mr. Halliday had a quiet night, after all. There were no admissions, and Mr. Porteous is coming down to see Mr. Wilson himself this morning.' Annette frowned and looked over Rebecca's shoulder as she studied the reports. 'Oh, and that boy David Phelps seems much easier this morning.'

Rebecca nodded. 'All right. Do you think his mother will come and see him today?' She bit her lip. 'Poor kid! She doesn't seem to care what happens to him.'

Annette shrugged. 'I guess being the mother of four children with no husband to bring in the lolly isn't exactly a picnic!'

Rebecca sighed. 'I suppose not. Where is the father?'

'Don't ask me, darling. He doesn't take me into his confidence.' She smiled ruefully. 'Snap out of it, Rebecca! We're not here as social workers, just as nurses, remember?' She patted her friend's shoulder. 'Heavens! I nearly forgot. You had a phone call yourself, just before you came in...'

Rebecca stared at Annette exasperatedly. 'Not Paul Victor again!'

'The very same.' Annette chuckled. 'And you called Barry persistent!'

Rebecca flopped down into the chair Annette had vacated. 'For goodness' sake, why does he persist in phoning me?'

'I guess he thinks he's in love with you.' Annette tilted her head to one side, smilingly.

Rebecca gave her an impatient frown. 'I'm almost six years older than he is,' she exclaimed.

'Honey, don't tell me, tell him.'

'I have.' Rebecca hunched her shoulders. 'Why ever did I allow myself to be hustled into going out with him in the first place?'

'Because he's handsome, and you liked him,' remarked Annette frankly.

'He's a boy!'

'And you're a woman, I know.' Annette giggled merrily. 'Honestly, Rebecca, you are a fool. You simply

can't see that you've got to be firm! All this letting
him down lightly! It doesn't work. Can't you see?'

Rebecca heaved a sigh. 'Apparently not.' She shook
her head. 'I did—I do like him. It's just that—well, he's
a little intense for me. And I guess I'm always conscious of the age gap.'

Annette moved to the door, looking back at her
doubtfully. 'It's not only the age gap, is it, though?'
She frowned 'It's something else; the something that
prevents you from taking seriously any of the men who
pursue you.'

Rebecca bent over the reports. 'Now, Annette——'
she began.

'Now, Annette—nothing!' Annette gave an exasperated snort. 'Sooner or later you'll have to take someone
seriously, Rebecca.'

Rebecca looked up. 'Why will I?'

'You want to get married, don't you? Have children?'

Rebecca shrugged her slim shoulders. 'Perhaps I'm
not the marrying kind.'

Annette wrinkled her nose angrily. 'Of course you're
the marrying kind! Heavens, haven't I seen you myself with those children down on Ward Six? You're
exactly the kind.'

'Isn't it time you were leaving?' asked Rebecca
pointedly.

Annette draped her cloak closer about her. 'You're
exasperating, do you know that?'

Rebecca smiled. 'I know. You've told me before.'

Annette stared at her for a moment longer and then
with a sigh she left the room. After she had gone,
Rebecca went and poured herself some coffee and over
the aromatic beverage she thought again about Paul
Victor. He was, as Annette had said, very persistent,
and although Rebecca liked him she wished he would
realise that so far as she was concerned he was wasting
his time. As a medical student here at St. Bartholo-

mew's, he could have had his pick of the nurses and student nurses, but for some inexplicable reason he had picked her. It was not so inexplicable really. Tall, and slim, and attractive, Rebecca found it all too easy to attract men, but she seemed indifferent to her appearance and to the men who asked her for dates. It was through Annette and Barry Morrison that she had met Paul. Barry, several years older and a houseman at St. Bartholomew's, had known Paul since their school-days, and in consequence had invited Annette's friend Rebecca and Paul to join him and Annette for dinner one evening. The evening had been a great success, and with some misgivings Rebecca had agreed to go out with Paul another evening, alone. It was then that she had realised how useless it was, and since, she had been trying to convince Paul of her decision. It was no good. She simply wasn't interested in men, and nor did she want to be.

Later in the morning, accompanying the surgeon, Mr. Porteous, round the ward, Rebecca encountered Paul Victor. He was with several other medical students and he signalled to her vigorously behind Mr. Porteous's back, creating a general feeling of amuse-ment among the other students. Rebecca compressed her lips impatiently. Annette was right. She would have to tell Paul firmly once and for all.

After the surgeon had gone, Rebecca returned to her office and was talking to the staff nurse when there was a knock at the door. Staff Nurse Williams went to open it, and she glanced round at Rebecca helplessly. 'It's Mr. Victor, Sister,' she said awkwardly.

Rebecca got up from her chair angrily. 'Paul, this has got to stop!' she exclaimed.

Paul hesitated, just inside the door, glancing pointedly at Staff Nurse Williams. 'Rebecca, I have to see you! Didn't you get my phone message? I asked Sister Fleming to tell you I'd phoned.'

Rebecca clenched her fists. 'Yes, Paul, I got your

message,' she replied shortly. 'But what you don't seem to understand is—this is a hospital ward, not a reception centre!'

Paul grinned. 'Come on, now, don't be stiff and starchy. When can I see you?'

'I've told you, Paul. I can't see you. I—I don't have time.'

Paul coloured. He was a handsome boy with thick curling dark brown hair and blue eyes. Most of the nurses thought he was dishy, but Rebecca was immune from that kind of romanticism. She had been cured of that three years ago...

'Why?' he asked now, apparently uncaring of Janet Williams' amused appraisal. 'You're finished at seven-thirty. Couldn't we have a drink together?'

Rebecca hesitated. She didn't want to accept any more invitations from him, but he was gradually becoming more persistent and she couldn't have him coming here to her office for obvious reasons. And in any case she could hardly speak to him here in front of Janet Williams.

'All right, all right,' she said, sighing. 'We'll have a drink. I'll have to go back to the apartment to change first, but I'll meet you at the Gridiron at eight-thirty.'

Paul's face lightened. 'Great! I'll see you!' He disappeared out the door and Janet closed it firmly and then met Rebecca's rueful gaze. Rebecca shook her head helplessly.

'What else could I do? He's impossible.'

'I think he's nice.' Janet gave a sigh. 'Why don't you want to go out with him?'

Rebecca shrugged. 'I don't know. We're too different, I suppose. Besides, I'm years older than he is.'

Janet secured a strand of hair that had come loose from her cap. 'Age means nothing these days,' she exclaimed. 'I wouldn't let that stop me. Not if I was interested.'

'It's not just that.' Rebecca gave an impatient gesture. 'I just don't want to get involved with—with anyone.'

Janet shrugged her shoulders. 'You could do worse. They say his family are simply rolling in money!'

Rebecca bent her head. 'Money doesn't interest me.'

'Doesn't it?' Janet wrinkled her nose. 'I wonder why?'

Rebecca shook her head. 'Oh, for goodness' sake, let's change the subject, shall we? I've had enough of Paul Victor for the present.'

Rebecca's apartment was in the older part of the town, the upper floor of a converted Victorian type dwelling. Although its plumbing was sometimes erratic and the paint was peeling on the landings she preferred it to the stark concrete and plate glass monstrosities which were springing up around the town centre. With emulsion paint, and a good deal of old-fashioned elbow grease, she had transformed the largest room into a colourful, comfortable lounge and its warmth and homeliness were welcoming after a tiring day. It was a place to retreat to whenever she felt the need; a place where she could be herself.

During the past three years she had needed a retreat many times and she had learned a great deal about herself in the process. She had had plenty of time to get over that disastrous affair in Fiji and looking back on it from the maturity of years she found she was able to pity Adele and her twisted malevolence. However, even now, she found it difficult to think of Piers St. Clair with any degree of detachment. Mostly, she tried not to think about him at all, and her work helped tremendously. Only sometimes in the dark reaches of the night it was impossible to deny the stirring shreds of the agony she had suffered.

When she had first returned to England, she had thought of Adele frequently, particularly as Adele herself wrote to her several times, pleading her forgiveness and begging her to return. She had replied to Adele's first letter, refuting all Adele's attempts at apology and asking her not to write again. When she had continued to correspond, Rebecca had burned the letters, unread, and eventually Adele had given up. Rebecca wanted no tenuous links with the past to mar whatever future she could carve out for herself.

It was two years since she had taken this position at St. Bartholomew's, and now she felt almost content; as content as she would ever be, she supposed. She got on well with her fellow nurses, and she had purposely gone out with several of the unmarried doctors in an attempt to rid herself of Piers' image. But most attempts had been unsuccessful and none of them had touched her deeply. She knew she was accused of being frigid, but it wasn't that. She supposed, in her most depressed moments, that she still loved Piers St. Clair, and she might as well accept the fact that nothing would change that.

Now she made herself a snack while she prepared to meet Paul, flicking through the clothes in her wardrobe with a critical eye. Already October was upon them and while the days remained mildly warm, evenings were definitely chilly. Eventually she chose a dark blue trouser suit, made of a woollen material that was both light and warm. Her hair, which she wore shoulder-length these days, tipped slightly at the ends, and she left it loose instead of pinning it into the neat pleat she wore at the hospital.

The Gridiron was in the centre of the town, one of the sleek hotels that provided casual eating facilities near the bar. When Rebecca entered the bar lounge, Paul was already there, sitting on a stool beside the bar, smoking a cigarette and toying with a whisky and soda. His eyes brightened when he saw her, and he patted the seat beside him encouragingly. Rebecca crossed the bar, and slid on to the stool at his side, ignoring the warm blue eyes which swept over her.

'What will you have?' Paul indicated the drink in his hand.

Rebecca frowned. 'Just a martini, I think, please,' she answered, and refused his offer of a cigarette as they waited for the barman to bring her drink. Cupping her chin on one hand, she surveyed the pseudo olde-worlde effect behind the bar enchanced by a trail of multi-coloured lights. 'I like this place, don't you?'

Paul shrugged. 'It's all right. I thought we might go on to the Prince Edward later for a meal.'

Rebecca bit her lip, and smiled rather absently at the barman as he delivered her martini. 'I don't think you understand, Paul,' she said carefully. 'I only arranged to meet you tonight so that I could ask you in rather more private surroundings than my office at the hospital to stop bothering me.'

Paul rested his elbow on the bar, and supporting his chin, regarded her tolerantly. 'That was kind of you.'

Rebecca couldn't suppress a smile. 'Well, honestly, Paul, six phone calls in the past fortnight, and this morning you actually put in an appearance! You didn't know who might have been in my office when you knocked. What would you have done if Mr. Porteous or Mr. Latimer had been there? Not to mention Dr. Hardy.'

Paul grinned. 'I should have produced some masterly piece of nonsense designed to allay the most suspicious mind.'

Rebecca sipped her martini exasperatedly. 'Don't you care that I've told you I don't want to meet you again?'

He chuckled. 'Not particularly. You're here tonight, aren't you?'

Rebecca had to concede that point and she shook her head helplessly. 'Paul, I'm five—almost six years older than you are. We—well—we have nothing in common.'

'Is that a fact?'

Rebecca shook her head. 'Well, anyway, I want you to stop pestering me. I like you—I think you're a nice boy—but I don't want to get involved with anybody.'

'So I hear.' Paul studied his drink thoughtfully. 'They say you had an unhappy love affair. Is that right?'

Rebecca's cheeks burned. 'Who are "they"?' she enquired coldly.

Paul shrugged. 'People. Men, mostly.'

Rebecca seethed. 'It's a pity *they* have nothing better to do then, that's all,' she exclaimed. 'Men—they're worse gossips than women!'

'Some are, some aren't,' remarked Paul. 'I notice you don't deny it.'

'Why should I? It's no business of yours whatever the truth of the situation, and I don't intend to satisfy your inquisitiveness!'

'Tell me about yourself,' he suggested softly. 'I am interested—not curious.'

Rebecca swallowed half her martini at a gulp. 'There's nothing to tell.' She glanced round. 'This bar gets very crowded, doesn't it?'

Paul sighed. 'Then let's go and have dinner.'

'I do not intend going any further with you than the door of this hotel!' retorted Rebecca heatedly.

Paul heaved a sigh. 'Why? What's wrong with me?'

Rebecca lifted her shoulders. 'Nothing—there's nothing wrong with you. It's simply that—well, you'd be wasting your time with me.'

Even as she said the words, Rebecca felt a strange sense of foreboding. She had said those words before—to Piers St. Clair.

'Let me be the judge of that.' Paul leaned towards her. 'There's no man in your life, I know that. Just let me be around. I won't ask anything that you're not prepared to give.'

Rebecca stared at him compulsively for a long moment, and then she looked jerkily down at her glass.

Why couldn't she accept his friendship? All right—he was young, but maybe that was in his favour. At least he could not accuse her of leading him on. She had made her position abundantly clear.

Sighing, she looked up. 'All right, Paul,' she said.

'All right—what?'

'All right, I'll have dinner with you.'

Paul's eyes brightened considerably. 'You will? Marvellous!'

Rebecca caught his arm. 'On my terms,' she said quietly.

'Agreed,' Paul nodded, and Rebecca bent her head. She had not committed herself, so why had this sense of foreboding increased? It was a peculiar sensation and she couldn't honestly find any reason for it except that for a brief agonising moment she had brought everything that had happened in Fiji to the forefront of her mind.

Much to Rebecca's surprise her friendship with Paul Victor was quite a success. They did not see one another often, but when they did their association with one another developed naturally into the casual companionship of friends, the kind of companionship Rebecca would not have thought possible between members of opposite sexes. He was well-read, and their tastes in literature and plays were similar. In the summer he enjoyed tennis and swimming, as she did, and he had told her that he had travelled all over the world with his father and consequently had enjoyed the benefits of a warmer climate in the depths of winter. Rebecca did not mention her own time in Fiji, even though she felt sure Paul would not have asked too many questions, but she did tell him more about herself than she had told any man. Occasionally now he came to her apartment, and if their relationship was frowned upon by some members of the hospital staff, it was jokingly speculated upon by others, and both opinions she ignored. Only Annette Fleming knew the real truth of the situation, and she encouraged her, thinking Rebecca knew, that eventually Paul might shake her out of her indifference.

One evening Paul met her from work in his car. It was drizzling, a chilly November day, with lowering skies and an icy blast in the wind. Rebecca was finished early and they planned to have a meal before going to the cinema. Over steak and french fried potatoes, Paul said: 'I found out today that my aunt's nurse knows you.

Rebecca looked up, startled. 'Your aunt's nurse?' she said questioningly. 'Who is that?'

Paul smiled. 'Sheila Stephens.'

'Sheila—Stephens!' Rebecca was incredulous. Sheila was the girl she had used to share a flat with; the girl who was going to marry Peter Feldman! She shook her head incredulously. That was all five years ago now, and Sheila had had time to get married and divorced. 'How—how is she?'

Paul shrugged. 'Fine.' He toyed with his fillet steak. 'We were discussing my work at the hospital and I happened to mention your name. She said you and she used to share a flat.'

'That's right, we did.' Rebecca hesitated. 'Actually, I thought Sheila was married.'

Paul shook his head. 'Not so far as I know. Naturally I don't know her well. I only see her occasionally. She seems a nice girl.'

'She is.' Rebecca cupped her chin on her hand. 'What a small world! Sheila Stephens!' She sighed. 'I'd like to see her again.'

'She would like to see you.' Paul pushed aside his plate. 'I said I'd arrange it.'

Rebecca smiled at him. 'That was thoughtful of you.'

'Yes, wasn't it?' Paul grinned. 'Seriously though, would you like to meet her?'

'Of course.'

'Then you'd better come to my house——'

'Your house?' Rebecca stared at him.

'Of course. My aunt lives with us—with my father and me, that is. My mother's dead, you know, I told you.'

'I know, but——' Rebecca spread her hands. 'I—I couldn't possibly come to *your* house. I mean—after all, Sheila is only your aunt's nurse——'

'That doesn't matter——'

'Of course it matters, Paul. Heavens, I have the apartment, she can come there.'

'Don't you want to see my home, is that it?'

Rebecca flushed. 'Don't be silly, Paul. But as I understand it your home is miles away, the other side of London, in fact.'

'So what? You have days off. We could make an outing of it. I'd like you to come.' Paul looked at her appealingly.

Rebecca sighed. 'Honestly, Paul, I thought you realised by now that our relationship——'

Paul lit a cigarette and drew on it deeply. 'I realise everything,' he said, blowing smoke rings into the air. 'I still want you to come. Heavens, where's the harm? I'm not fooling you, you know. Your girl-friend is there!'

Rebecca pressed her lips together. 'Oh, I believe that,' she said uncomfortably. 'It's just that—well—your family——'

'There will only be my aunt there. My father's abroad somewhere. He spends very little time in England, actually. Besides, I'd like you to see the house. My father bought it about fifteen years ago. It's one of those old Georgian country houses, standing in its own grounds.'

Rebecca bit her lip. Of course she had known that Paul's family were wealthy, but somehow the thought of going to his home brought it more significantly to mind, and she really wished she could refuse. But as Paul said, it would make a pleasant trip, and she would like to see Sheila again. She traced the pattern of the tablecloth absently. Then she looked up to find Paul's eyes upon her, his expression hopeful.

'I don't know, Paul,' she began slowly. 'I—well—I'd hate your family to get the wrong impression about us.'

Paul stubbed his cigarette out impatiently. 'Why should they?'

'I don't know. I just feel——' She shook her head. 'If—if you lived in a semi-detached in Cricklewood, I wouldn't mind so much, but a Georgian manor house——'

Paul hunched his shoulders. 'Look, Rebecca, I can't help it if my father's family, and my mother's family come to that, made a fortune out of industry, can I? That side of the coin doesn't interest me. That's why I left home and took this medical degree. I was always pretty bright,' he said this without false modesty, 'and I guess physics and chemistry had always interested me. In any event, I entered university without difficulty and went on from there. I want to be a doctor, not a general practitioner, you understand, but some kind of specialist. I'm interested in children's diseases, and pediatrics seems my most likely destination. I'm telling you this so you'll realise that I'm not wanting to take you to *Sans-Souci* to blind you with wealth and possessions, to try and persuade you by material means.'

Rebecca linked her fingers together. 'I'm sorry, Paul,' she said softly. 'Of course I'll come.' Then she frowned. '*Sans-Souci!* Unconcern. That's an unusual name for a house.'

Paul shrugged. 'It was my mother's idea,' he said, beckoning the wine waiter. 'It was typical of her attitude to life.'

There was bitterness in his voice as he spoke, and

Rebecca felt a sense of compassion for him. It was obvious that whatever benefits he had had, a happy home life seemed not to be one of them.

They drove down to *Sans-Souci* a week later. It was Saturday, and Paul had arranged to take the same weekend off as Rebecca. Whether he planned that they might stay the night at his home, Rebecca wasn't sure, but she was determined to insist on returning that night. Either that, or putting up at a hotel.

They skirted London, driving into the Hertford-shire countryside. This was a part of England Rebecca did not know well, even though she had lived in and around London all her life. They stopped at Har-penden for lunch and drove on into Buckingham, arriving at the village of Linslow soon after two-thirty. It was a pretty place with thatched cottages lining the main street. There was an olde-worlde inn, and the grey stone church spire rose above stark elms, silhou-etted against a sky that showed sometimes blue, some-times cloudy grey. The bare trees around the village green still sparkled with traces of frost, and although the sun shone in snatches it was very cold.

Paul glanced at Rebecca smilingly, noticing her pleasurable reactions, and said: 'It's like another world, isn't it?'

She nodded. 'I imagine though that people who live in villages like this have more social life than some town dwellers. I mean—everyone knows everyone else, don't they, and there's a spirit of camaraderie, isn't there?'

Paul gave her a wry smile. 'I suppose so. It cuts both ways, though. You simply can't keep secrets in villages, and if you have something to hide, heaven help you!'

Rebecca frowned. 'You say that as though you had.'

Paul shook his head. 'Oh, no,' he said. 'At least—not now!'

Rebecca pondered this remark as they drove

through the village and took a narrow private road that wound for some distance between skeletal trees before reaching a barred gate marked Private. Paul opened the gate, drove through, and closed it again, and he smiled at Rebecca as he slid back into the car. 'As you can see, I'm a true countryman,' he remarked mockingly. 'I always close gates behind me.'

Rebecca smiled with him and looked ahead with interest. Now she could see acres of rolling parkland on either side of the drive and ahead of them as they breasted a rise she saw the house.

She didn't know quite what she had expected, but certainly nothing so imposing as the porticoed facade of *Sans-Souci*. It stood against a backdrop of hills, gaunt and magnificent, with two octagonal towers rising to either side of the central mass. Corinthian columns shadowed the entrance above a flight of shallow steps, giving the building a slightly Grecian appearance.

Rebecca looked questioningly at Paul as they drove up to the massive forecourt where, incongruously, a sleek grey Mercedes was parked. Paul, sensing her eyes upon him, glanced at her half ruefully. 'Don't you like it?'

Rebecca gave an expressive gesture. 'That's not the point, is it? Heavens, this is like some Palladian mansion.'

Paul chuckled. 'I suppose it is. I've lived here so much I guess I don't notice it any longer.'

He brought the car to a halt at the foot of the steps leading up to the pillared entrance, and Rebecca climbed out rather reluctantly. Smoke spiralled from chimneys and somewhere dogs barked, heralding their arrival. On all sides stretched acres of undulating land, dipping and rising and thick with belts of trees, all bare now in the bleakness of autumn. The house itself had the atmosphere of years upon it, and unaccountably Rebecca shivered.

Immediately Paul took her hand and led her up the steps. 'At least its appointments are not as ancient as its walls,' he commented encouragingly, and shaking her head she allowed him to lead her inside.

Paul closed the door behind them and Rebecca looked about her curiously, unable to deny the interest the house had aroused in her. As Paul had said, inside was vastly different from outside, and she couldn't decide whether she liked it or not. The hall, which had once been an enormous apartment, had been divided into two, and arched ceilings had been lowered. Central heating had been installed and the floors were thickly carpeted. Only the huge fireplace flanked by stucco sculptures seemed typically Georgian in design.

As Paul removed his overcoat and helped Rebecca out of her sheepskin jacket a manservant appeared from a doorway across the hall and came to greet them. Dressed in a dark suit, his greying hair thinning on top, he could have been a member of the family, thought Rebecca, except for the old-fashioned deference he showed to Paul.

'Good afternoon, sir,' he greeted him politely.

Paul nodded and smiled. 'Hello, Gillean. Where is everybody?'

Gillean cast a curious glance in Rebecca's direction, and then said: 'Your aunt and Nurse Stephens are in her suite, sir. Oh, and your father is back from Amsterdam.'

'Oh! Is he?' Paul sounded surprised and Rebecca looked quickly at him.

'Would you rather we came back some time when your father is not at home?' she asked, uncomfortably, and he shook his head vigorously.

'Heavens, no,' he exclaimed. 'I just didn't expect my father to be here, that's all. Actually, I'm glad he is. I'd like you to meet him.'

Rebecca smiled. 'All right. If you're sure he won't mind.'

'Mind?' Paul regarded her with amusement. 'My dear girl, you aren't the first girl-friend I've brought home.'

Gillean took their coats and said: 'Have you had lunch, sir? Or would you like Mrs. Gillean to make you both a meal?'

Paul shook his head again. 'Oh, we've eaten, thank you, Gillean. By the way——' He took Rebecca's hand and drew her forward. 'Rebecca, I'd like to introduce you to Gillean. He's my father's head of the household, an old-fashioned title, but apt, don't you think?' He smiled. 'His family have been here since the early nineteenth century when they served the original owners of the house, the Harmondseys. Lord Harmondsey was the lord of the manor, I suppose, in those days, and it was quite an honour being in service here.'

Rebecca smiled and shook hands with the elderly manservant while Paul told him that he and Miss Lindsay would go up and see his aunt. 'Where is my father, anyway?' he enquired.

'In the study, sir,' answered Gillean, at once. 'He brought Mr. Bryant home with him, and as I understand it they are studying the plans of the Australian project.'

Paul bent his head. 'Oh, Tom Bryant, yes.' He considered for a moment, and then he said: 'Well, you can tell him we're here when you get the chance, but we'll go on up to see my aunt. Miss Lindsay is a friend of Nurse Stephens.'

'Very well, sir.' Gillean stepped aside and Paul led Rebecca across the pile-carpeted hall to where a spiral-staircase had been installed which led up to a wrought-iron balustraded gallery.

'The original staircases were in the towers,' Paul informed her, as they climbed. 'But it is so much more convenient and attractive to have a staircase in the hall, and in any case my mother liked to make an entrance.'

Rebecca digested this, making no comment. She thought the idea of staircases in the towers was quite a romantic one, but she said nothing.

The house was automatically in three sections. There was the bulk of the building which formed the central portion, and the west and east wings which jutted out beyond the towers at either side. Paul explained that in years gone by the lower part of the west wing had been wholly taken over as servants' quarters with the kitchens being there also. But now that staff was so hard to come by, most of that part of the building was unused, and only the stables which adjoined the kitchen quarters were fully occupied. His father, he said, had his suite of rooms at the back of the house in this central portion, while his aunt and himself occupied the east wing.

'It's far too big, of course,' he observed, wiping a film of dust from a window ledge. 'Mrs. Gillean has only two helpers, a girl who comes daily from the village and Mrs. Fellowes, whose husband is the gardener. She tackles the rough work, Mrs. Gillean herself does most of the cooking.'

To Rebecca, who had never known the luxury of even a housekeeper, it all seemed rather awe-inspiring, but she successfully hid any trepidation she might be feeling and thought instead of the pleasure it would be to see Sheila again.

They walked along a corridor whose windows overlooked the sweep of forecourt before the house and the long narrow gravelled drive. For all Paul might find dust on the window ledges and spiders' webs in some of the corners, the whole place was luxuriously carpeted and furnished, and obviously great care had been taken to make it very comfortable.

Paul stopped outside double white panelled doors

and after a light tap entered the room. Rebecca followed him, looking about her with interest. The room was high-ceilinged and attractive, with pink damask-covered walls and a cream and gold carpet underfoot. It was furnished as a lounge, with deep chairs and couches upholstered in striped satin. A wide window-seat overlooked the side of the house and the village in the distance. As in the other apartments, the heating was provided by long low radiators, and the log fire that crackled in the grate was more for effect than anything else.

As the room was deserted, Paul called: 'Aunt! Aunt Adele! Are you there?'

And even as Rebecca's features froze in the semblance of a smile, there was the swish of a chair's wheels and a woman propelled herself forward into the room through an open doorway. Thinner than even Rebecca remembered, her emaciated features twisting in amused mockery, it was unmistakably Adele St. Cloud, and for a moment Rebecca felt quite faint. Then common sense asserted itself and the memories that had suddenly crowded her shocked mind receded. Adele was regarding her intently, obviously deriving a great amount of pleasure from Rebecca's startled reactions, and it came to the girl that Adele had known she was coming.

'Well! Well!' Adele spoke first. 'So this is the young woman we've been hearing so much about, Paul!'

CHAPTER TWO

REBECCA stiffened and Paul glanced at her curiously. 'Yes,' he said, in answer to his aunt's question, and then to Rebecca, in an undertone: 'Are you all right, love? You look awfully pale.'

His solicitude was soothing and Rebecca was glad of it. His hand at her elbow was warm and reassuring and for the first time in their relationship she needed him. 'I—I was surprised to meet your aunt, that's all,' she said now. 'You see—we do know one another already, don't we, Miss St. Cloud?'

Paul looked puzzled and looked to his aunt for confirmation. 'Is that right, Aunt Adele? Do you know Rebecca?'

Adele chewed her lower lip, apparently taken aback by Rebecca's sudden shift to the attack. Until then she had held all the cards. 'Yes, it's true,' she agreed. 'Rebecca was my nurse in Fiji.'

'Good lord!' Paul was amazed, though not at all perturbed, regarding this as an amazing coincidence. 'How amusing!'

'Yes, isn't it?' Adele looked fully at Rebecca. 'You're looking well. A little thinner perhaps, but aren't we all?'

Rebecca managed to smile. She would not allow Adele to notice her consternation. But her mind was in a whirl. So many questions manifested themselves, so many anxieties probed her consciousness. That Adele St. Cloud should be Paul's aunt was absolutely incredible. She had never imagined Adele might return to England. Somehow whenever she had thought of her it had been in Fiji. And Paul must be the son of one of her sisters. She remembered Adele had said she had several. And as Paul had told her that his mother was dead, possibly his mother had been called—Denise; yes, that was the name Adele had used, Denise.

Adele watched the girl with cold, calculating eyes, and Rebecca wanted nothing so much as to turn and run. It wasn't that Adele frightened her; it was simply that she wanted to have nothing to do with any branch of this family.

Paul, sensing nothing amiss, said: 'Where's Sheila? Rebecca and she were close friends years ago.'

'Were they?' Adele raised her eyebrows. 'How nice! Well, she'll be back soon enough. I think she's exercising the dogs at the moment.' She patted the chair nearest to her. 'Rebecca, my dear, come and sit with me and tell me what you've been doing with yourself all these years.'

Rebecca hesitated. She had no desire to sit down beside Adele with or without Paul's comforting presence. But Paul urged her forward and she moved reluctantly across the room to Adele's side, perching on the edge of the chair near her. It was as though time had shifted back three years and she shivered momentarily.

Adele, seeing that involuntary shudder, said: 'You're cold, Rebecca. I'll have Gillean make up the fire.'

Rebecca shook her head. In a cream tweed slack suit she was anything but cold; apprehensive, that was all. 'It doesn't matter,' she said quickly, and looked appealingly across at Paul who was lighting a cigarette now.

Adele looked at her nephew, too. 'Where's your father?' she enquired, with casual interest.

Paul shrugged. 'I haven't seen him yet, but Gillean said he was in his study. I hear he's brought Tom Bryant back with him.'

Adele nodded. 'Yes. They've been in Amsterdam together.' She turned appraising eyes on Rebecca's controlled countenance. 'You must tell your father that Rebecca is here, Paul,' she said. 'I'm sure he would like to meet her again. They became great friends when he was in Fiji. You remember Piers St. Clair, don't you, Rebecca?'

Rebecca stared at Adele incredulously, seeing the bitter blue eyes flash with malicious amusement. She had the awful premonition that Adele had planned all this—but she couldn't have! And yet how could it be true? Paul's name was Victor, not St. Clair. She turned tormented eyes in Paul's direction, but fortunately he was looking at the newcomer who had just entered the room, a small, attractive redhead, dressed in a simple white uniform and cap.

'Hello, Sheila,' he greeted her warmly. 'Rebecca, look who's here!'

Rebecca felt her legs would not support her. She had never been the fainting kind, but she was no longer sure of her immunity. Piers St. Clair was *here*, in this building, downstairs! Oh, God, she had got to get away, she thought sickly, before she made an absolute fool of herself and passed out completely.

Sheila, unaware of her tension, crossed the room to where Rebecca and her patient were sitting. 'Hello, Rebecca,' she said, smiling, and Rebecca wondered if it was her imagination or merely the desperate state she was in that made her think the smile did not quite reach her eyes. 'What fun to meet you again. After all these years.'

Rebecca forced herself to stand up, and smiled weakly at Sheila Stephens. 'Oh, Sheila!' she exclaimed. 'When Paul told me you were his aunt's nurse, I couldn't believe it. How are you?'

Sheila glanced briefly down at Adele. 'I'm fine, Rebecca,' she responded easily. 'Miss St. Cloud is not a difficult patient to care for—as no doubt you know.'

Rebecca's eyes flickered. 'Oh—oh, yes!' She frowned. 'You knew I'd worked for her in Fiji?'

'Of course.' Sheila bent to her patient, smoothing the cushion which supported her back, asking her if she was comfortable. Then she straightened and Rebecca had the most ridiculous idea that she was looking at a stranger. 'Miss St. Cloud and I are great friends, aren't we?' She smiled at Adele conspiratorially.

Adele chuckled, 'Indeed we are!'

Rebecca linked her fingers through the strap of her handbag. 'How—how long have you been here, Sheila?'

Sheila frowned. 'About eighteen months, I suppose.'

'When my mother died, Aunt Adele came home to England to stay for a while,' explained Paul, joining their conversation. 'That was just before Sheila applied for the position, wasn't it, Aunt Adele?'

Rebecca swallowed hard. Of course, her confused mind insisted, Paul's mother was dead. And if Piers was his father—— She swayed a little, catching the back of the chair for support, but not before Sheila had noticed her distress.

'Is something wrong, Rebecca?' she exclaimed.

Paul was immediately all concern. 'Something is wrong, Rebecca,' he insisted, putting an arm about her shoulders, supporting her. 'Come along, let's go and get some air. This is a stuffy room.'

Rebecca nodded, but Adele intervened, 'Don't you think it would be more sensible if Sheila took her friend to her sitting room for a while, Paul? I'm sure they have plenty to talk about, and after all, that is why Rebecca came, isn't it?'

Paul hesitated. Rebecca wished she could think of some excuse to go with him instead of Sheila, but of course she could not.

'Is that what you'd like to do, honey?' he asked.

Rebecca sighed. 'I—I suppose so,' she conceded awkwardly.

Paul's arm tightened about her for a moment leaving her in no doubt as to his feelings, and then he let go and said: 'Okay, Aunt Adele. I'll go and see my father. Then we'll all have tea together later.'

Adele looked delighted and Rebecca thought bitterly that she had won yet another small victory. Even so, she had come with the intention of spending some time with Sheila, so perhaps she was being uncharitable. But Adele must know exactly how she was feeling, having exploded the bombshell about Piers upon her. With slightly unsteady legs, she followed Sheila out of the room and along the corridor to her own sitting room. This was a large attractive apartment with a bedroom adjoining, and Sheila had added to the already luxurious appointments. There was a television, and even a small electric hotplate on which she could prepare herself light meals. Several articles of clothing were strewn about the room, reminding Rebecca vividly of her untidiness at the flat, but these garments were obviously far more expensive than those she had used to possess five years ago, and Rebecca wondered whether Sheila was being influenced by her surroundings.

Sheila indicated that she should sit down and Rebecca complied, glad to be off her legs. 'We'll have some coffee, shall we? You look as though you could do with some. Was it such a shock seeing Adele again?'

Rebecca stretched her fingers along the upholstered arm of the chair, searching for something to say in reply. 'I—I suppose it must have been,' she agreed, wishing she could relax. But her thoughts were tearing her apart and she felt sick and giddy.

'It was Adele's idea,' Sheila was going on. 'Keeping her identity a secret, I mean. When she found out I knew you she was very interested.'

I'll bet she was, thought Rebecca tortuously, compressing her lips tightly. How Adele must have delighted in this opportunity to see her—her victim—again. She tried to think, but it was difficult to be coherent, even in her thoughts. *Paul was Piers' son!* That particular manifestation superseded all others and destroyed any vulnerable hopes she might have had for the future.

Sheila added instant coffee to the cups and turned as she waited for the kettle to boil. 'Aren't you going to ask me how I like private nursing?'

Rebecca nodded. 'Of course. Do you like it here?'

Sheila nodded vigorously. 'I love it. I didn't know whether I would, but I do. Everyone's so kind and—friendly.'

'I suppose you know Paul's father, too?' Rebecca could not suppress the words.

Sheila smiled. 'Piers? Of course.'

Rebecca coloured. Sheila had said his name deliberately, she was sure of it.

Sheila seemed to be studying her closely, watching for her reactions, and with deliberate cruelty, Rebecca brought up the one subject she had wanted to avoid. But she had to distract Sheila somehow.

'I—I thought you would have been married by now,' she remarked. 'To Peter.'

'Peter Feldman?' Sheila uttered a scornful exclamation. 'You didn't seriously imagine I would marry him after your soulful gesture, did you?'

'What do you mean?' Rebecca's surprise at Sheila's tone of voice was sufficient to banish for a moment the agonising problems that had suddenly arisen. 'I thought you loved Peter.'

Sheila turned to pour the boiling water into the cups. 'I did—or at least I thought I did.' She swung round. 'You didn't actually believe you were fooling anyone, did you? Good God! Peter wasn't the type to indulge in clandestine affairs if you were! His face was always sickeningly expressive!' There was harsh bitterness in Sheila's tone now and Rebecca felt terrible.

'Oh, Sheila——' she began, shaking her head.

Sheila controlled her features and handed her a cup of the steaming liquid. 'Sugar?' she asked politely.

Colouring, Rebecca helped herself to a spoonful of

sugar, and then as Sheila came to sit opposite her, she said: 'I don't know what to say, honestly.' She sighed helplessly. 'I thought—we both thought——'

'I know, I know!' Sheila sounded impatient. 'Look, let's drop it, shall we? I'll accept your gallant gesture for what it was.'

Rebecca pressed her lips together. 'I'm sorry,' she said inadequately.

Sheila shrugged. 'Don't be. You did me a favour really. I realised soon afterwards that I would never have been happy with a man like Peter Feldman. He was too tolerant; too easily led. I prefer a man who's capable of being master in his own home.'

Rebecca bent her head and sipped her coffee. Dear God, she thought shakenly, if only I had never come here how much easier life would have been.

Sheila drank her coffee in silence and then rose to put the cups into the small washbowl which adjoined the small stove. Rebecca looked about her, trying desperately to think of some way to relieve the tension. It was incredible to believe that she had looked forward to seeing Sheila again only to find her changed beyond recognition. Was it only because of Peter, or was this yet another example of Adele's destructive influence?

When there came a knock at the door, both girls turned simultaneously, and for a moment Rebecca was terrified that it might be Piers. But Paul entered the room at Sheila's bidding and grinned at them with refreshing innocence. 'Hello,' he said. 'Is this a private party or can anyone join?'

Sheila's expression was warm as she looked at him. 'Would you like some coffee, Paul?' she asked.

'No,' he shook his head. 'I was only joking. Actually, tea is served in Aunt Adele's sitting room and she asked me to let you know.' He looked with rare tenderness at Rebecca. 'Are you feeling any better?'

In truth Rebecca felt as though her nerves were stretched to breaking point, but she managed a faint relieved smile and said: 'I'm much better, thank you.'

'Good.' Paul pulled her to her feet and for a moment held her close, his lips brushing her hair. But Rebecca was supremely conscious of Sheila's eyes upon them, and she hastily pulled away, smoothing her suit.

She was a mass of nerves as they walked along the corridor to Adele's room. She dared not ask Paul whether he had seen his father, for she felt sure now that Sheila was aware of her previous relationship with Piers. How she knew this, she did not know, but obviously Adele had used her as a confidant. But apart from Adele, there was no one else in her sitting room.

'I told my father we were here,' Paul volunteered as they entered the sitting room. 'But he didn't take any notice. He and Tom are engrossed on the Australian project.'

Adele smiled. 'Never mind, dear boy, there's plenty of time to see your father. You're staying for dinner, of course.'

'Oh, but——' began Rebecca, eager to get away, only to find Paul interrupting her.

'Yes, we can stay,' he said firmly. 'Actually, I wondered if we might stay the weekend, eh, Rebecca?' His eyes pleaded her indulgence.

Rebecca shivered. 'We can't, Paul,' she said, gripping her tea cup with both hands.

'Why?' Adele's eyes regarded her piercingly. 'Paul told me you had both got the weekend off.'

'We have ... that is ... oh, *Paul*!' Rebecca stared at him appealingly, willing him to intercede.

But Paul seemed unwilling to appease her, and the matter was left there. Sheila, sensing the tension, broke it by saying: 'I expect you found it hard to adapt to life in England again, Rebecca. After Fiji, I mean.'

Rebecca hesitated, and then sighed. 'I—I suppose I did.'

Adele surveyed her mockingly. 'I never could understand why you decided to leave, Rebecca,' she said. 'I thought you liked it there.'

Rebecca bit hard at her lower lip. 'I expect I was tired of such a confined existence,' she responded, using anger to hide her uncertainty.

Adele flushed at this and Sheila took up the conversation again. 'I've never been to the south Pacific. I expect the weather is marvellous.'

'Of course.' Rebecca looked down at the liquid in her cup, and to her relief Paul took up the conversation, asking about his aunt's health and telling her how he was getting on at St. Bartholomew's. Presently, his tea finished, he rose and said: 'How would you like a walk in the grounds, Rebecca? It's getting dark and I'd like you to see something of the place.'

Rebecca bit her lip. She wanted to insist that they leave now, but obviously this wasn't the place to do it when Paul had his aunt as an ally, urging him on. So she smiled and said: 'Yes, I'd like that,' and they left the room.

They walked back along the corridor and reached the head of the spiral staircase as two men emerged from a doorway below them. Rebecca stiffened, and shrank back against the wall of the gallery. Paul, unaware of her trepidation, ran lightly down the stairs, expecting Rebecca to follow him.

'Hi!' he said, as he reached the hall, and attracted his father's attention. 'Have you finished?'

As Rebecca held tightly to the balustrade she saw Piers St. Clair turn and smile at his son and her heart leapt as though it would choke her. In a dark lounge suit, his thick hair only lightly tinged with grey at the temples, Piers St. Clair was as attractive as ever, and if his body seemed leaner than she remembered, it only served to toughen his appearance. He moved with a lithe, easy grace of movement, and as though it were yesterday she could recall with clarity the hardness of his body against hers on the bed ...

Oh, God! she thought, trembling sickly. Don't let

him look up here and see me! The notion was ridiculous; *stupid*! Any moment now Paul would look round to introduce her and then—— She heaved a shaken breath. Obviously when Paul had told his father of their arrival, he had not been explicit about his companion, but what did it matter when sooner or later they were bound to come face to face?

Realising it would be better to assume a calmness she didn't feel rather than to cower here like some ravaged maiden, she began to descend the staircase, and even as she did so Paul glanced round to find her.

'Come on, Rebecca,' he said, smiling caressingly. 'I want you to meet my father again.'

Whether or not Paul had mentioned to his father that he already knew the girl he had brought with him, Rebecca did not know, but even in the shadowy depths of the hall she sensed the sudden urgency of Piers' eyes upon her, and heard his bitten-off ejaculation.

For her own part, she did not look at him until she was actually on ground level, and approaching him across the vast expanse of turkey red carpet. Then she saw the cold, incredulous bleakness of his eyes, and the hard line of his mouth as he shook his head almost imperceptibly.

The man beside him was a relief to look upon. Tom Bryant was not as tall as Piers, and thicker set, with crisp brown hair and tanned broad features. He was smiling at Rebecca, knowing none of the undercurrents present here this afternoon, and her gaze clung to his to avoid that other ruthless appraisal.

'Well, Father,' said Paul, drawing Rebecca forward and placing a casual arm about her shoulders. 'You remember Rebecca Lindsay, don't you?'

Rebecca had, perforce, to look at Piers now, and she was shocked by the cruelty she saw in his face. 'Yes,' he said, at last, his accent as attractive as ever, 'I remember Adele's nurse.'

Rebecca allowed him to take her hand but drew hers away swiftly. Touching him was too bitter-sweet, for her, if not for him. She broke into nervous speech, saying the first thing that came into her head: 'But, Paul, your name is Victor—not St. Clair.'

'My son's name is Paul Victor St. Clair.' Piers spoke coldly. 'When he joined the staff of the hospital, it was considered too much, so it was abbreviated.'

'Oh! Oh, I see.' Rebecca shivered at the bleakness of Piers' eyes. But Paul seemed to notice nothing amiss, for he turned to the other man saying:

'Rebecca, let me introduce Tom Bryant, my father's right-hand man. Tom—this is Rebecca Lindsay. She also works at the hospital, but she used to be Adele's nurse. She met my father when he was out in Fiji.'

Tom Bryant relieved the tension. He shook hands with her warmly, enclosing her slender fingers in his large ones, and commented upon it jokingly. Rebecca responded to his humour eagerly; anything to avoid Piers' piercing mental dissection. They stood for a few moments longer discussing their work at St. Bartholomew's and then Piers said:

'I suggest we adjourn to the library. We can have a drink there.'

'I was just about to show Rebecca the grounds,' said Paul.

'It's almost dark,' observed Piers shortly. 'I suggest you leave that until the morning.'

Paul looked at Rebecca. 'We could do that,' he murmured.

Rebecca clenched her fists. 'You forget, Paul, we won't be here in the morning.'

Piers looked at her intently. 'Surely my son has invited you to stay the weekend? Besides, it's getting quite foggy. It would be madness to attempt to drive back to London tonight.'

Rebecca's lips froze and she looked wordlessly at Paul. 'You can't blame me for the weather, honey,' he remarked innocently, spreading his hands.

Rebecca twisted her gloves. 'But I'm not—prepared,' she protested. 'Surely we can get back to town?'

Paul looked impatient. 'Why should we? There's plenty of room here.'

'Paul, before we came——'

'I think we can consider the matter closed,' said Piers suddenly in a bored tone. 'You cannot leave to-night, so you might as well accept it. Now, shall we have that drink?'

Rebecca pressed her lips together angrily. It was bad enough that Paul should take this method of getting his own way without the positive awareness that Piers St. Clair considered she was behaving childishly. And there was nothing she could do, short of making a scene, so she allowed Paul to take her arm and guide her across the hall to the library in silent resentment.

Piers St. Clair opened the door and she had to pass him to enter the room. As she did so she was supremely conscious of him and despite her anger her legs were slightly weak. Then she deliberately directed her attention to her surroundings, finding the booklined room exactly how she imagined a library should be. The room overlooked the gravelled forecourt of the building, for this room was at the front of the house. The heavy drapes at the windows were of dark green velvet, as were the upholstered armchairs that were scattered about the room. Again here a log fire spluttered in the grate casting leaping shadows upon the walls. Piers put on tall lamps which only partially dispelled the illusion, and Rebecca thought how much she could have appreciated it if there had been no disturbing tensions to mar her enjoyment.

Paul seated her near the fire and joined his father at a cabinet set in the wall which contained a varied assortment of spirits. Rebecca watched them together, noticing the similarities between them which hitherto had not occurred to her. They were not alike in looks or build, but although Paul's eyes were blue and his father's very dark, they had the same shape, the same long length of lashes. He moved like his father, effortlessly, and his hair grew in the same way. They both had long-fingered hands and now that she knew they were father and son she noticed a certain familiarity of manner, of attitude, of indolence almost.

'What would you like, Rebecca?' asked Paul, studying the contents of the cabinet. 'Whisky, gin, vodka? Or just a martini, perhaps.'

'A martini would be fine,' agreed Rebecca automatically, and Paul poured the vermouth and handed it to her. He and Tom Bryant both had whisky, while Rebecca noticed that Piers poured himself a generous measure of brandy. She recalled what he had said once, at Adele's house, in Fiji, when he had chosen brandy, and she wondered rather desperately whether his equilibrium had been upset this afternoon.

Tom seated himself near her, and said: 'What do you think of *Sans-Souci*, Miss Lindsay?'

Rebecca was glad she had the glass in her hands to occupy her attention. 'It's—very impressive,' she said awkwardly. 'Paul didn't warn me, I'm afraid. I imagined something less spectacular.'

Tom smiled, leaning forward in his seat, taking a drink of his whisky. 'Yes, I thought as you did. After all, there are very few of these places still privately owned. Most are put into the hands of the National Trust.'

Piers came to stand before the fire, his back to the flames. 'I have decided to sell the house, Tom,' he said, rather harshly.

Tom looked up in surprise. 'Have you? Well, you've talked about it long enough.'

Piers shrugged. 'It is an expensive white elephant,' he said. 'Besides, as you know, I never cared for the place.'

Paul looked at Rebecca. 'My mother chose *Sans-*

Souci,' he said, by way of explanation. 'When she was alive she was always giving parties here. She loved entertaining, didn't she, Father?'

Rebecca gave Piers a hasty glance, wondering how he would react to Paul's casual chatter. But Piers seemed indifferent to his son's observations, and Rebecca found herself wondering about Jennifer St. Clair.

Tom took up the conversation again, speaking to Paul now, and from time to time Rebecca felt Piers' eyes upon her. She wondered what he was thinking; what construction he had placed on her presence here; and inwardly quivered. She found herself speculating about him, wondering whether, now that Jennifer was dead, he intended marrying again. From his attitude towards her it was painfully obvious that whatever he had felt for her in Fiji had been a fleeting thing, and her agony all these years had been self-inflicted.

They were interrupted by someone knocking at the door and when Piers called: 'Come!' Gillean entered the room. He addressed his master although he glanced towards Paul for confirmation. 'I've had the green room made up, sir. Is the young lady staying the night?'

Rebecca glanced angrily at Paul who had the grace to colour self-consciously, but Piers gave no attention to either of them. *'Oui,* Gillean,' he said shortly. 'Miss Lindsay is staying the night. And perhaps it would be a good idea to show her her room now.'

Rebecca rose abruptly. She did not want to stay; she wanted to walk out of this room, out of this house, and never come back, but that was impossible. Besides, it would be running away again...

'Thank you, Gillean,' she said, through taut lips. 'I would like to go to my room.'

'Rebecca?' Paul sounded anxious.

Rebecca looked at him scornfully. 'I'll see you later, Paul,' she said briefly, and with a husky: 'Excuse me!' she walked out of the room.

Gillean followed her and then indicated that she should follow him. Rebecca managed a faint smile at the elderly servant. It wasn't his fault after all, and she should not be uncivil to him. They crossed the hall and passed through a heavy oak door into the passage beyond, and Rebecca realised they were in one of the towers. Gillean began to climb the spiral staircase, and she went after him, pausing now and then to peer through the narrow windows that appeared at intervals. They emerged on to a landing, and Gillean pushed open the door of one of the rooms, allowing her to precede him inside.

Now Rebecca looked round with undisguised pleasure. It was a charming room, octagonal in shape and illuminated by wall lights which Gillean had switched on as he opened the door. The carpet which penetrated every corner of the room was pale green tumble twist while the bedspread and curtains were a slightly darker shade of brocade. Gillean watched her reactions politely and then said: 'Your bathroom adjoins this room, miss. Unfortunately the rooms are not inter-communicating, but you do have this part of the building to yourself.' He smiled.

Rebecca gave an involuntary gesture. 'It's marvellous, thank you, Gillean,' she said.

Gillean nodded. 'I'm glad you like it, miss. Is there anything else you'll be wanting?'

Rebecca hesitated a moment. 'I don't think so, Gillean. What time is dinner?'

'Usually about seven-thirty, miss. Mr. St. Clair—he has a drink in the library before the meal—where you were a few minutes ago. Perhaps you could join the family there about seven-fifteen.'

'Oh, yes, I see,' Rebecca nodded. 'Do I go down the same way we came up?'

'No, that's not necessary, miss. Look here.' He led the way back on to the landing and indicated the two doors. 'That door is your bathroom and this other one leads into the main gallery. This used to be the usual way into the main building.'

'Oh, I see,' Rebecca said again. 'Thank you.'

Gillean nodded and smiled again. 'There's plenty of hot water if you'd like to take a bath anyway. I'll leave you now.'

'All right.' Rebecca managed a responsive smile and he left her. Then, when it was no longer necessary to behave unnaturally, she closed the door and sank down on the bed, burying her face in her hands.

Of course, eventually she had to get up again and she went into the bathroom and stripped off all her clothes. As Gillean had said, the water was boiling and she ran herself a deep bath in the porcelain tub which could have held four adults comfortably. There were bath salts, too, and she scented the water liberally and lay in its perfumed depths for a long time. Somehow the heat of the water banished the coldness inside her and she refused to consider the evening ahead. It was something to face and get through and there was no point in anticipating disaster.

Even so, she could not prevent herself from thinking about Piers St. Clair. It was at once an agony and an ecstasy to think of him when for so long she had denied him entry to her conscious mind. So long he had been there in her subconscious without the power to penetrate the numbness in which she had enfolded herself. But now he would not be denied and a curling pain of anguish tore at her stomach. Paul had said his mother was dead, so that meant that Piers was a widower. She recalled with clarity the cruelty of his expression as he had looked at her this afternoon and knew without a shadow of a doubt that that fact meant nothing to him so far as she was concerned. On the contrary, he had treated her as though he found her presence in his house distasteful . . .

She wondered what he thought her relationship with his son was. And she also wondered whether it was part of Adele's plan to reveal to Paul exactly what her relationship had been with his father. Rebecca shivered, even in the hot water. It was terrifying to realise how destructive Adele could be.

She was in her bedroom applying mascara to her lashes when there was a knock at her door. With trembling fingers she put the mascara brush aside and called: 'Who—who is it?'

'Me! Paul!'

Rebecca felt suddenly weak with relief, but she felt no gratitude towards Paul because of that. It was his fault they were here at all, and certainly his fault that they were committed to staying the night. 'What do you want?' she called impatiently.

Paul heaved an exaggerated sigh. 'Open the door, honey. I want to see you.'

'No.' Rebecca put the mascara away. 'I'm not fully dressed yet. I'll see you at dinner.'

'But I want to explain——'

'There's nothing to explain, Paul. Just go away.'

'Oh, Rebecca, please! Let me see you.'

Rebecca hesitated, and then she stood up and reached for her trousers. Buttoning them round her slim waist, she pulled on the jacket and went resignedly to the door. Opening it, she confronted Paul who was looking particularly attractive in a dark dinner jacket.

'You realise I can't dress for dinner, don't you?' she said, rather shortly. 'Honestly, Paul, you planned all this, didn't you?'

Paul stepped into the room, glancing round with interest. 'No, I didn't plan it. How could I plan a fog?'

Rebecca sighed. 'Well, anyway, I just wish we could have stayed in the village.'

'That would have aroused comment,' observed Paul dryly.

'I don't particularly care,' retorted Rebecca tautly.

'Why? Don't you like it here? Is it Aunt Adele? I know she can be trying at times.'

Rebecca controlled her colour. 'No—no, nothing like that.' She bit her lip. 'Did—did your father know I was coming?'

'How could he? He was in Amsterdam.'

'Oh, yes.' Rebecca compressed her lips.

Paul looked at her curiously. 'What's wrong, Rebecca? You've seemed edgy ever since you came here. Is it something I've done?'

Rebecca coloured now. 'Of course not.' She glanced at her watch. 'It's seven-fifteen. Oughtn't we to be going down?'

Paul came close to her. 'You're beautiful, do you know that?'

Rebecca moved to the door. 'Oh, not now, Paul,' she said, a trifle impatiently, and Paul gave her a pained glance.

'What's wrong with me?' he exclaimed. 'You freeze up every time I get near you.'

Rebecca shook her head. 'I thought we understood one another.'

'We do—that is—all right, Rebecca. I'm sorry. I guess I've loused up your weekend altogether, haven't I?'

Rebecca relented. 'No—no, it's not you. It's me,' she replied, sliding her hand through his arm. 'Shall we go down?'

CHAPTER THREE

THE library seemed filled with people all of whom turned to regard the newcomers, Rebecca thought, as she and Paul entered together. And yet there were only four other people present: Adele, Sheila, Tom Bryant and Piers. Of all of them, Tom's face was the most friendly, and Rebecca was glad he was there.

Sheila, in a soft clinging gown of lemon chiffon, looked quite startlingly attractive, and Rebecca wondered why she should feel so surprised to see her there. After all, when she had been Adele's nurse she had often dined with her patient, and if in this instance the circumstances were different, given that this was not Adele's house, why should it matter?

Adele, herself, seated regally in her wheelchair, seemed poised to enjoy some inner amusement, and Rebecca felt repelled by her avid expression. But in spite of that, in spite of Sheila's beauty, in spite of Tom Bryant's cheerful countenance, it was to the other man that Rebecca's eyes were compulsively drawn.

Piers St. Clair looked darkly handsome, his linen immaculate, his dinner jacket sleek and expensive. He looked every inch the successful man he was, and Rebecca wondered however she had had the temerity to treat him as she had done. He was like a stranger, and although her nerve ends tingled when she looked at him, she could hardly believe he had once held her in his arms and made passionate love to her.

'Ah, there you are, Paul.' Adele was the first to speak. 'We were beginning to think you were not coming down.' Her words were blatantly insinuating and Rebecca felt her colour rising. She was glad when Piers turned away, saying:

'What will you both drink?'

Paul glanced at Rebecca, raising his eyebrows, and on impulse, she said: 'I'll have a brandy and soda, Paul.'

Piers did not look round but merely measured out their drinks and Paul went to take them from him as he turned. Sheila, sipping a glass of sherry, looked at Rebecca curiously, and Rebecca wondered what construction she was putting on all this.

Piers lit a cheroot and Tom Bryant said: 'The fog's much thicker. Has anyone been outside?'

'No.' Paul listened with interest. 'Is that a fact? I guess you'll have to stay, too, Tom.'

'Tom was staying anyway,' remarked Piers, inhaling deeply. 'How are things at the hospital, Paul? Did you give Harrison that information?'

'Yes.' Paul moved to his father's side. 'He was interested. He asked whether you thought the project was feasible.'

Piers bent his head, listening to his son with frowning concentration, and Rebecca felt bereft. Until that moment, she had not realised exactly how much she was relying on Paul's support, and to have it removed, even to the other side of the room, was rather devastating.

Tom Bryant moved to her side before Adele could engage her in conversation, and he offered her a cigarette smilingly. 'You look pretty anxious,' he observed. 'Was it so important that you should get back to town tonight?'

'What? Oh—oh, no, not really.' Rebecca pressed her lips together. 'It's simply that I wasn't prepared ...' She glanced down ruefully at her cream trouser suit.

Tom chuckled. 'Without wishing to sound affected, Rebecca; I may call you that, mayn't I?' and at her nod, he continued: 'I would say that what you're wearing is adequately appealing. You're one of the few women I know who can wear trousers attractively.'

'Thank you.' Rebecca smiled at him warmly. 'You've no idea how much you've helped me.'

Tom shrugged. 'It's not difficult to be pleasant to someone like you.' He glanced down at her slim fingers. 'You're not married?' He shook his head. 'That surprises me.'

Rebecca bit her lip. 'Marriage isn't everything.'

'No.' Tom inclined his head in agreement. 'I'm not married myself. However, I am a slightly different proposition. My work takes me away a lot. It wouldn't be fair to expect a woman to live the kind of nomadic life I lead.'

'I expect if a woman loved you, she wouldn't mind,' remarked Rebecca gently. 'After all, one can't always map out one's life and expect it to follow a given course, just because you direct it so.'

'You talk with feeling—is that from your own experience?'

'I suppose it is.' Rebecca sipped her brandy and soda. 'Oh, this is good. Do you like brandy, Tom?'

'No, whisky's my ruin, I'm afraid. You should talk to Piers. He's quite an expert on cognac. His family come from the wine-growing areas.'

Rebecca was glad of the excuse of the brandy to account for the suddenly heated skin of her body. Tracing her finger round the rim of her glass, she said: 'You've known—Paul's father for a long time, I suppose?'

'God, yes.' Tom nodded. 'And you met him some time ago, too. Out in Fiji when Piers visited Adele, is that right?'

Rebecca trembled a little. 'Yes—that's right,' she agreed, glancing round awkwardly. But no one was listening to their conversation. Piers and his son had separated and now Paul was talking to his aunt while his father was handing Sheila another glass of sherry. Sheila looked up at Piers with limpid blue eyes, holding his gaze with her own for what seemed like a long moment. Rebecca felt her heart begin to pound heavily and she looked quickly away. Surely not, she thought, nauseously. Surely Piers wasn't involved with Sheila! And yet why not? Why should she be surprised? She had only been Adele's nurse when she had attracted his attention. She closed her eyes for a brief period and when she opened them again she found Tom regarding her with obvious concern.

'Are you all right?' he was asking, frowningly. 'You look very pale suddenly. Is something wrong?'

Rebecca shook her head, bringing the colour back into her cheeks. 'I felt a little faint, that's all,' she excused herself. 'It's very close in here.'

Tom continued to watch her anxiously. 'Are you sure?' he persisted. 'I thought you looked rather strained earlier on. Perhaps you're working too hard. I imagine your work is quite demanding for one so young.'

Rebecca tipped her head to one side, concentrating on what Tom was saying to the exclusion of everything else. 'I find nursing a very rewarding occupation,' she said now. 'The hours are long and sometimes inconvenient, I suppose, but I don't go out a lot, so I don't mind.'

'And what about all these parties nurses are always throwing? I understood there was plenty of social activity within a hospital.'

Rebecca smiled. 'I'm afraid parties are not my metier. I'm rather an isolationist, I suppose. I enjoy listening to music, and reading——'

'Oh, come on, Rebecca!' The shrill tones deriding what Rebecca had just said startled her, and she swung round to confront Sheila who had walked over to listen to their conversation now. 'You always used to love entertaining. We gave dozens of parties at the flat when we shared.'

Rebecca flushed. 'That was some time ago, Sheila.'

'I know that, but a person doesn't change so completely. Heavens, even in Fiji I understand you used to go out quite a lot.'

Rebecca stared at her for a moment and then her eyes shifted to Adele who had wheeled her chair silently across to join them. 'I think you've made a mistake, Sheila. I didn't go out at all when I was nursing Miss St. Cloud.'

Adele's eyes narrowed. 'Well, maybe not often, eh, Rebecca?' She glanced at Tom. 'It rather depended who invited her, of course.'

Rebecca felt mortified. Did Adele intend bringing Piers' name into the conversation? Piers himself was pouring another drink and seemed entirely indifferent to their group. But Paul's curiosity had got the better of him and he joined them, putting a casual arm across Rebecca's shoulders, much to her annoyance.

'What's going on?' he enquired easily.

There was a moment's awkward silence, and then a knock at the door disturbed them. It was Gillean to announce that dinner was served and Rebecca couldn't suppress the sigh of relief which escaped her.

Piers took charge of Adele's chair, wheeling her out of the library, and as Tom was already with Rebecca Paul was forced to walk with Sheila. Dinner was served in a panelled dining room that could have accommodated thirty people comfortably. As it was, they were all seated at one end of the long polished table to avoid the inevitable difficulties which would have ensued had they taken up the whole length of it. The table appointments were exquisite; lace place mats, obviously designed in Venice, were the base for silver cutlery, bone china, and crystal glass. There was a central piece of red roses interlaced with lacquered green leaves, and each napkin was folded to resemble a rose.

Piers took the chair at the head of the table naturally, with Adele to his left and Tom to his right. Rebecca was seated beside Tom, while Paul found himself opposite her between his aunt and her nurse. The situation did not please him, Rebecca could tell, but to some extent she was relieved. Tom had taken Paul's place temporarily as a shield between Piers and herself, and he had the added attraction of not presenting any emotional involvement.

The meal was delicious; the main course was roast duckling and despite Rebecca's nervousness she found herself talking to Tom and eating almost unthinkingly. There was a raspberry mousse to follow and then coffee was served in the adjoining lounge. This was one of the smaller rooms of the house, and its furnishings were mostly contemporary, apart from a carved cabinet in one corner in which resided a collection of jade which attracted Rebecca's interest. While Adele took charge of the coffee cups and talked to her nephew and to Sheila, Rebecca walked over to the cabinet and was standing admiring a particularly unusual chess set when she became conscious that someone had come to stand beside her. She glanced up, expecting to see either Paul or Tom, only to find it was Piers. Immediately tenseness overtook her and with it a trembling sense of inadequacy.

'*Eh bien*, Rebecca, and what do you think of my house?' he asked, his voice cold and somehow scathing.

Rebecca rubbed her elbows nervously with the palms of her hands. 'It's very—well—imposing,' she replied awkwardly.

'You think so? I should have expected a different reaction from you. Tell, me, did you know I was to be home this weekend?'

Rebecca frowned. 'What do you mean?'

'What I say. Did you expect to see me, or did you perhaps hope to—to familiarise yourself with the building before my return?' His eyes bored bleakly into hers.

Rebecca blinked. 'I didn't even know it was your house until I met Adele,' she said, in a taut angry tone.

His eyes narrowed. 'You do not expect me to believe that, of course.'

'Why not?' Rebecca quivered a little.

'Paul is my son, Rebecca.'

'So?'

'So—it is obvious! It is inconceivable that he should not have mentioned his family.'

'He—he did! But not by name.' Rebecca moved away from him, bending to examine a jade figurine and Piers moved too, much to her dismay.

'You expect me to believe that you did not know who Paul was?'

Rebecca straightened, breathing swiftly. 'I don't particularly care what you believe,' she said huskily, unable to accept this coldness from him.

Piers stared at her grimly. 'You, of course, know nothing about Halliday!'

Rebecca's brows drew together in bewilderment. 'Halliday?' she echoed blankly. 'Who is Halliday?'

Piers uttered an exclamation and drew out his cheroots, putting one between his teeth to light it. 'We will leave it for the moment,' he snapped harshly, glancing round to find that while no one could hear what they were saying their conversation was being observed. Through his teeth he muttered: 'Do you think you are the only one with the prerogative to be cruel, is that it?'

Rebecca's face burned. 'Please,' she said, feeling rather sick having this confrontation after such an unusually rich dinner. 'I don't know why you're talking to me like this. I came here to meet Sheila, that's all. Do you think if I'd known Adele was to be here I'd have come?'

Piers studied her for a long moment, and then bent to light his cigar. 'I don't know what your game is,' he said bitterly, 'but I refuse to believe your motives were as innocent as you imply.'

Rebecca swallowed hard, wondering however she

was going to face Adele after this. It made her wonder exactly what Adele had said about her after she had gone.

'Piers!' Adele's voice broke into her thoughts. 'Piers, what are you and Rebecca talking about so earnestly? Paul's looking quite put out, aren't you, darling?'

Piers left Rebecca to walk lazily across the room. 'We were discussing the chess men,' he replied indolently. 'I was merely telling Rebecca that I bought them with the house.'

Rebecca knew it was expected of her to join them and act naturally, but it was terribly difficult when her emotions were so badly disturbed. However, she managed to cross the room and take the seat beside Paul, returning his smile automatically. Sheila looked at her curiously, and then looked at Piers. He met her gaze calmly, his dark eyes enigmatic, and Rebecca wondered what thoughts were going through his mind.

Paul stroked the back of her hand as it rested on her knee. The others had taken up the question of Piers' intention to sell *Sans-Souci* and for a moment they could have been alone. 'Tell me,' he said, frowning, 'how well did you know my father in Fiji?'

Rebecca stared at him incredulously, then she managed a casual shrug. 'Reasonably well,' she temporised. 'What time are we going back to town tomorrow?'

Paul chewed his lower lip. 'Aunt Adele told me at dinner that my father knew you worked at St. Bartholomew's. Have you seen him since—since you left Aunt Adele's house?'

Rebecca's nails bit into the palms of her hands. 'Of course not, Paul,' she replied honestly, while her mind raced on confusedly. What was Adele trying to do now?

Paul nodded. 'I guess he found out when he contacted them at the time I began my training,' he said, almost to himself. 'I'm surprised he never tried to see you. After all, Aunt Adele did say you were good friends.'

Rebecca sighed. 'I shouldn't take too much notice of what your aunt says about me,' she said carefully. 'She was rather—annoyed when I left her employment.'

'Why did you?'

Rebecca shook her head. 'Your aunt is not the easiest person to get along with, Paul.'

Paul smiled, some of the anxiety lifting from his face. 'I wondered what it was. Perhaps it would have been better if she had told me that she knew you, then I could have warned you.'

'Y—yes.' Rebecca was doubtful. Would she have come anyway? It was a doubtful possibility, and yet why should she have assumed any more than she did this afternoon that Paul's father might be Piers St. Clair?

Sheila came to sit beside them, regarding Rebecca intently. 'Have you got a nightgown or pyjamas with you? I could lend you something to wear.'

Rebecca smiled, trying to be charitable, even though she had the distinct impression that Sheila knew exactly what had passed between Piers St. Clair and herself in Fiji. 'That's all right, Sheila. I can manage. But thanks for the offer.'

Sheila shrugged indifferently. 'Never mind. When do you plan to go back to town, Paul?'

'In the morning, I guess. I doubt whether I'll be able to persuade Rebecca to stay longer.' He looked at Rebecca with gentle warmth.

Rebecca bent her head. 'We'll have to go anyway. We're both on duty first thing Monday morning.'

Sheila wrinkled her nose. 'Hospital work! How ghastly! I don't know how you could go back to it, Rebecca. I shouldn't like to.'

'That's because you like the material things of life, Sheila,' observed a sardonic voice, and Rebecca looked up into Piers' face again.

Sheila took no offence at his words, however, but

merely laughed softly, and said: 'I know I do. Why not? You pay me such a generous salary, you're making me a sybarite.'

Rebecca compressed her lips as Piers smiled at Sheila's impudence. 'I can always cut it,' he remarked, mockingly, and she rose to look into his face more closely.

'But you won't,' she said appealingly. 'Will you?'

Piers gave her a lazy smile. 'No, I won't,' he agreed, appraising the attractive picture she made with indolent ease. 'Do you feel up to a game of bridge? Your patient insists that you join her.'

A faint flicker of annoyance crossed Sheila's face just for a moment, and then she shrugged and walked across to Adele obediently. Piers surveyed his son and Rebecca.

'How about you, Paul?' he asked.

'No, thanks.' Paul was abrupt.

Piers frowned. 'And you—er—Rebecca?'

'I don't play.' Rebecca didn't look up.

Piers studied them for a moment longer, and then with an impatient flick of his fingers he too walked away to join Adele and the others.

Paul looked expectantly at Rebecca. 'Let's go to the library,' he suggested. 'My father has some excellent hi-fi equipment. We could play records.'

'All right,' agreed Rebecca, and they rose to leave the room. The others were setting up a table for bridge, but although Adele and Sheila watched their departure both Tom and Piers seemed engrossed in handling the cards.

It was very pleasant in the library, and Rebecca enjoyed looking through the pile of records, seated cross-legged on the floor beside Paul. But when he began to get close to her, sliding his fingers along her wrist, and nuzzling her neck with his lips she got up and left him.

She went to the window, peering through the heavy

drapes, rubbing a circle of clarity in the misty pane of the glass. Outside, the fog pressed its fingers close against the windows and only the faint outline of a tree near the house bore any resemblance to reality. They might have been cut off from time and space, floating in a void, without point or destination.

She sighed and closed the curtains again just as the telephone began to ring. Paul went to answer it, giving their number automatically, and listened as whoever it was on the other end imparted their message. His face changed as Rebecca watched and he frowned deeply. Finally, he said: 'All right, all right. I'll tell him,' and rang off.

Rebecca raised her eyebrows questioningly, and he shook his head unsmilingly. 'That was Harman, my father's bailiff. There's been a crash on the top road, near the north boundary. A car and a wagon of some sort.'

Rebecca moved forward. 'How awful! Is anyone hurt? Is there anything I can do?'

Paul's frown deepened. 'I must tell my father. Harman thinks one of the men is dead. Three people were involved, I believe.'

Rebecca nodded. 'I'll come with you.'

Paul hesitated, and then nodded. 'Okay,' he agreed, opening the library door.

The others were in the middle of a rubber, and Piers looked up rather impatiently, Rebecca thought, when Paul attracted his attention. He was partnering Sheila while Adele was Tom's partner, and it seemed obvious from the annoyance on Sheila's face also that they were winning.

'There's been a crash,' said Paul. 'On the top road. Did you hear the phone, it was Harman. He says they've ploughed through the fence in the copse. One of the men is dead——'

But Piers was already on his feet, flinging his cards aside. '*Bien, bien,*' he said grimly. '*Allons!*'

'I'll come with you,' said Rebecca, as they started across the room. 'I am a nurse. There may be something I can do.'

Sheila got to her feet. 'I'm a nurse, too.'

Piers regarded Sheila for a long moment. 'It would be a pity to ruin that dress,' he observed sardonically. 'Besides, Adele may need you. I'm sure—Rebecca will be perfectly adequate for what is needed.' He glanced at Rebecca without warmth. 'Do you need a coat? Paul—you go to the kitchen and ask Gillean for some lamps. I know he has some. Did Harman say he had called the ambulance—or the police?'

'Yes, of course. His cottage is quite near there, as you know. He had called them before calling us.'

'Good! Come!'

Leaving the warmth and light of the lounge, they crossed the hall to the heavy front door. Paul went on to the kitchen quarters while Piers pulled open the door and stepped outside. At once the thick mists swirled inside and with it the icy chill of freezing air. He glanced back at Rebecca and then crossed to the hall closet, extracting her sheepskin jacket and a similar one for himself. He threw the coat at her and she caught it deftly and pulled it on, refusing to allow his attitude to influence her now.

They descended the steps to the forecourt where the Mercedes still waited, and Piers thrust open the passenger door. 'Get in,' he commanded abruptly, and Rebecca complied, wondering whether Paul would object to being relegated to the back seat.

On the back seat was a pile of rugs and Piers came round and got in beside her, turning to thrust them to one side. A few seconds later Paul came running down the steps to join them, and as the rear door was open he climbed in.

The powerful engine roared to life, and they moved away smoothly, turning away from the drive up which Rebecca and Paul had driven earlier and taking instead an inner track which curved round the house and then continued across the parkland. Rebecca could see nothing to either side of this track, and only the orange fog lamps cast any illumination ahead of them. The road was rough in places, not gravelled like the drive and forecourt, and Paul, leaning forward and resting his arms along the back of the front seat, said: 'This used to be the bridle path until Harman widened it with his Land-Rover.'

Piers concentrated on his driving, and Rebecca's eyes were drawn to his hands on the wheel, visible in the lights of the dashboard. The wheel slid expertly through his fingers and she knew an aching desire to have those hands touch her again, to linger against her flesh with caressing tenderness. As though aware of the wantonness of her thoughts, Piers glanced at her at that moment, and she was overwhelmingly glad of the anonymity of the gloom inside the car. At least he could not read her expression or see the revealing colour in her cheeks.

Presently they slowed and Paul said: 'Almost there. This is the belt of trees I mentioned. Harman said the car had been parked in the copse and had pulled out in front of the wagon. When the wagon hit it they both skidded across the road and into the trees.'

Piers shook his head. 'Did he know who was in the car?'

'Yes. Michael Meredith—and Diane Howarth.'

'I see.' Piers chewed at his lip. 'And it's Michael who's——'

'Yes.'

'*Mon Dieu!* The idiot!' Piers sounded incensed.

'He's probably dead, Father.'

'But his wife is not—and it is she who will have to bear the brunt of this, *n'est-ce pas?*'

'I guess so,' Paul nodded, and Rebecca frowned. It seemed pretty obvious that the dead man had been parked with a woman who was not his wife and that was why Piers was so scathing. She frowned to herself. How could he judge this man so arbitrarily when he himself had indulged in just such an affair with her? She looked at his profile, grim and unyielding, and wondered why it was that of all the men she had known he should be the one who could not be displaced.

The car drew to a halt and now in the encroaching gloom the naked light of a broken tail-light could be seen. A man came out of the mist towards them, past a strangely unreal mound of metal which had once been Michael Meredith's saloon car. Piers had got out, and now the others did likewise, joining him as he spoke to the bailiff, Harman.

'What's going on?' he was asking, and Harman was explaining that the lorry driver was shaken, that was all, and was presently drinking tea from a flask which Mrs. Harman had brought along for him.

'It can't have been his fault,' went on the bailiff. 'The car just came out of the copse in front of him and he hadn't a hope in hell of pulling up. And the road's so narrow at that point that he couldn't avoid them without ploughing into the trees himself. As it was, he hit the front of the vehicle, and I guess Michael was killed instantly.' He ran a hand over his forehead as though to rid himself of the memory of what he had seen. 'Bloody awful mess!' he muttered.

Rebecca moved forward. 'What about the woman? Is she alive?'

Harman nodded vigorously. 'Yes, she's alive all right. But she's in a pretty poor way.'

'Miss Lindsay is a nurse,' Piers advised him suddenly. 'Maybe she could have a look at Diane.'

Harman looked doubtful. 'Are you sure——' he began.

'I'm not squeamish, if that's what you mean,' said Rebecca calmly, the urgency of the situation banishing temporarily her tenseness. 'Where is she?'

'Over here.' Harman led the way past the smashed car to where a body was lying half on the road and half on the grassy verge in the shade of the heavy trees. The dampness of the fog had overlaid her clothes with dew and Rebecca realised that until the ambulance came she must be kept warm. In the light of their torches and of the lamps Paul had got from Gillean it was possible to see the pallor on her face, and when Rebecca knelt and touched her hands they were frozen.

'Blankets,' she said, looking up at the men. 'Piers! Those blankets—or rugs in the back of your car. Could you get them?'

Piers nodded abruptly and turned and strode away, while Rebecca examined the girl. She had a nasty-looking wound on her head that seeped blood on to the ground around her, and a bone protruded from her arm just above the elbow. Apart from these injuries she was a mass of minor cuts and bruises, and there was a puffy swelling beside her ear. Rebecca wiped the blood from her face with her handkerchief, and tried rather unsuccessfully to make a pad of it to press over the wound. Glancing round, she said: 'Do either of you men have a handkerchief?

They both had, and she made a thick pad and pressed it firmly over the wound on the girl's head. Then, as Piers returned with the rugs, she gently but firmly eased them round her, wishing the ambulance would come quickly. It was quite possible that one of her legs was broken, and she might have any number of inner complications that could not be diagnosed out here on a foggy road.

Piers went to speak to the lorry driver and Rebecca got up and said: 'Where is the other man?'

Harman moved restlessly. 'Still in his car, miss. You don't want to see him, do you? There's nothing you can do.'

Rebecca sighed. 'There might be. I must be certain.'

Harman looked at Paul for guidance, but Paul

129

merely shrugged, and with obvious reluctance, Harman showed her the way over to the mangled wreck. After a brief glance Rebecca turned away. Harman was right; no one could help Michael Meredith now.

Presently the whining of a siren came to their ears and Piers came striding back to them. 'That sounds like the ambulance. That chap over there'—he indicated the lorry driver—'he'd better go with them to hospital. He's badly shaken up.'

'Yes, sir,' Harman nodded politely. 'You can go on home if you like, sir. Leave this to me.'

'I'd like to stay and speak to whoever they send out with the ambulance,' said Rebecca at once. 'They may need help.'

Paul sighed. 'Oh, come on, Rebecca. This is ridiculous! I'm frozen. There's nothing else we can do.'

Piers frowned at his son. 'If you want to go, take the car,' he said impatiently. 'I will bring Rebecca home in Harman's Land-Rover.'

'Like hell you will!' Paul hunched his shoulders. 'Come on, Rebecca! I could use a drink—something short and strong!'

Rebecca pressed her lips together. 'No, Paul, I'll stay here. You—you go back, as—as your father says.'

Paul stared at her angrily. 'What do you hope to prove by staying here? That you're as efficient as they are?'

Rebecca flushed. 'Don't be silly, Paul.' She knelt down beside Diane Howarth again. 'I just don't like leaving her, that's all.'

'Well, blast you then!' muttered Paul childishly, and stamped off towards the car, muttering to himself. Rebecca bit her lip, looking up into Piers' face anxiously, and he said:

'I must apologise for my son. I have the feeling he is allowing his imagination to run away with him.'

'What do you mean?' Rebecca frowned, glancing at Harman who seemed oblivious of them as he lit a cigarette.

Piers shook his head grimly. 'Later,' he said briefly, and went to watch for the ambulance.

It was all over quite quickly. The police arrived and as the inspector knew Piers he seemed to act with greater speed and efficiency. Firemen arrived to free what was left of Michael Meredith from the ruined car and the ambulance whined away with its three casualties. Floodlights were set up and the whole mangled mess was revealed to their appalled eyes. The lorry was lodged partially in the ditch at the side of the road and the men from the fire service, assisted by Harman and Piers, tried to lever it out. But in spite of their equipment it was awkwardly placed, and a certain amount of physical manpower was required to help the machinery.

Rebecca watched anxiously. This was something she had not expected, and seeing Piers half in the ditch, thrusting his shoulder against the heavy mass of the tipped lorry, was frightening. There was a moment when the whole thing seemed certain of collapsing on top of him, but then with a lurch it moved and swung almost effortlessly out into the road. Rebecca breathed a sigh of relief, and Piers vaulted out of the ditch rubbing his shoulder with his other hand.

'I think that's it,' he said, his gaze flickering over Rebecca before resting on Harman. 'Where is the Land-Rover, Harman? I'll send Baines back with it in the morning.'

'Just parked along here, sir,' indicated the bailiff respectfully. 'I'll hang on until these chaps go and then I can give you a full report in the morning.'

'Fine,' Piers nodded, lines of strain appearing on his face. '*Eh bien*, come along, Rebecca. We will go.'

They walked in silence down the track to the vehicle, and Piers slid behind the wheel almost thankfully. Rebecca looked at him curiously. During the last few minutes he seemed to have lost all his energy, and she wondered whether he had strained himself pushing the lorry.

However, he started the Land-Rover and turned it quite expertly before driving back past the wreck and on down the track towards *Sans-Souci*. He seemed to be driving with one hand only, however, and Rebecca's suspicions increased.

'Are you all right?' she asked finally, and he gave her a brief glance.

'*Naturellement,*' he replied bleakly. 'I expect you are cold.'

'No, I'm not cold. This coat is very warm.' She sighed. 'Piers, are you sure you're all right? You would tell me if something was wrong?'

Piers' fingers tightened on the wheel. 'And what would you do?' he asked tautly.

'I'm a nurse,' she answered impatiently.

He uttered a scornful exclamation. 'Of course! I had momentarily forgotten.' He leant forward staring through the windscreen. 'This damn fog seems to have thickened.'

Rebecca heaved a sigh. It was obvious that whatever was wrong with Piers he was not going to confide in her. She wondered why she should feel so hurt. After all, Sheila was waiting at the house. No doubt he would rather consult her if something was wrong. She chewed at her lips. She had got to stop thinking like this. The sooner she got away from here the better.

Piers brought the car to a halt at the side of the house, and they entered through a door set in the wall which led into a small hallway where wellington boots and mackintoshes were stored, along with golf clubs and other sporting equipment.

Rebecca waited for Piers to shed his sheepskin coat, but he did not, merely indicating the door which led into a passage which in turn led into the main hall. 'You go ahead,' he said abruptly, and she pressed her lips together and walked quickly across to the door.

But as she reached it she happened to look back and her breath caught in her throat as she saw the agony on his face.

'Piers', she exclaimed tremulously. 'What's that stain on your coat?'

He raked a hand through his hair impatiently. 'For God's sake, go!' he muttered through clenched teeth. 'Do you think I want you to see me like this! *Go!*'

CHAPTER FOUR

REBECCA ignored him and dragged off her own coat, throwing it aside carelessly. Then she went across to him, touching the stain on his coat and feeling its sticky warmth. 'In heaven's name, Piers,' she cried unsteadily, 'what have you done?'

Piers shook his head grimly. 'I don't need your pity,' he muttered violently. 'It's just a cut, that's all. That damn lorry was torn to ribbons!'

'Oh, Piers!' Rebecca stared at him helplessly. 'Please —take off your coat. Let me look at it!'

Piers hesitated a moment longer, and then he unfastened the jacket and pulled his good arm free of it. It was obvious from the strain on his face that it was agony to remove the other sleeve. His dinner jacket came next, and Rebecca was horrified by the amount of blood he had lost. But she said nothing, knowing that any inconsequential remark from her might prevent him from allowing her to examine him. Finally he unfastened his shirt, pulling it free of his trousers, his eyes constantly watching Rebecca's expression.

His chest was tanned and muscular, and liberally covered with hairs, and Rebecca tried not to be aware of him as a person as she examined his shoulder. But it was terribly difficult when the heat of his skin was so close to her and her whole body ached for a closer contact.

The wound was in the flesh of his upper arm, but although it bled copiously it had not severed the main artery. 'I need some water and antiseptic—and some bandages,' she said at last, her hands unsteady. 'Do you have any?' She shook her head. 'You really should see a doctor.'

'There's a first aid cabinet in my bathroom,' he said huskily. 'Will you go there?'

Rebecca moved away, wiping her hands on a paper tissue she had taken from her handbag. 'I—I suppose so,' she agreed.

'Or would you rather I asked Sheila to do it for me?' he asked, his eyes mocking her.

Rebecca turned away. Even in pain he had to hurt her.

Lifting his clothes, he slung them over his good shoulder and then indicated that she should precede him along the passage. When they reached the tower stairs he said: 'We'll go this way. I do not particularly wish to attract attention to myself.'

'Very well.' Rebecca preceded him upstairs, glancing round now and then to make sure he could make it. He was very pale, but his eyes glittered grimly, and she knew he did not really care for her helping him. The wound should really be stitched, she thought anxiously, wondering whether it was possible for her to obtain an anti-tetanus serum and administer it here. He obviously did not care whether he was poisoned or otherwise—but she did . . .

He staggered as they reached the top of the stairs and on impulse, she said: 'My bedroom's here. You stay here and I'll go and get the bandages myself. Just tell me where to go.'

He regarded her contemptuously. 'Thank you, but I prefer my own room,' he said, fighting off waves of dizziness. 'It's not much further——'

But even as he spoke, his knees buckled and he collapsed on the small landing.

Rebecca gasped and went down on her knees beside him, but he was unconscious. The amount of blood he had lost allied to the tremendous amount of strain he had put on himself had robbed him of his strength and he lay there helplessly, the blood seeping from his wound into the carpet.

She knew she couldn't cope alone, and with a reluctant look at him she hurried back down the stairs, seeking the kitchen quarters and Gillean. Asking him to avoid alerting the household yet, she asked him to call Mr. St. Clair's doctor and then between them they carried the unconscious man into the bedroom which had previously been allotted to Rebecca. While she waited for the doctor's arrival, Rebecca sponged the wound clean and put on a dressing which Gillean brought to her. He acted on her orders without question and she thought how understanding he was. He didn't ask unnecessary questions, nor did he get in the way. He simply helped her as quickly and as efficiently as he could.

Of course, when the doctor arrived, Adele demanded to know what was going on and Paul came out into the hall to confront Rebecca impatiently.

'Gillean says my father is unconscious upstairs—in *your* room!'

Rebecca coloured. 'That's right, he is. Oh, Paul, it's a long story, and one I can't tell right now. He was hurt at the scene of the accident, that's all, and he collapsed.'

Paul shook his head and Adele who had wheeled herself out of the lounge to hear the tail-end of their conversation, said: 'And why wasn't I told immediately, instead of you taking over and behaving in this underhand manner? You're nothing in this house, miss, not even a member of the staff, so don't think you can give orders here!'

Rebecca sighed. The doctor was mounting the stairs and she wanted to go with him, to be there when he examined Piers, to explain what had happened. 'Look,' she said, 'I didn't want to worry you, that's all. Your brother-in-law was helping the men to get the lorry out of the ditch and has torn his shoulder. He collapsed on his way upstairs.'

'To *your* room?' Paul was furious.

'No, of course not.' Rebecca's cheeks were scarlet. 'For goodness' sake, Paul, this isn't the time or the place to be arguing about what happened.' She glanced towards the stairs. 'I must go. Excuse me.'

Turning, she ran across the hall and up the main staircase leaving Adele to stare after her impotently. But Paul followed her, and behind him came Sheila Stephens.

Shaking her head, Rebecca crossed the gallery to the door which led into the tower landing. Her bedroom door stood wide and she found Doctor Mortimer in the process of undressing the wound. Piers had recovered consciousness, and was himself looking at the doctor with impatient eyes.

'*Mon Dieu*, Mortimer,' he exclaimed, as Rebecca came into the room. 'You are wasting your time here. I don't need a doctor!'

Doctor Mortimer turned to look at Rebecca, and Rebecca looked at the doctor, avoiding Piers' accusing eyes. 'I understand from Gillean that you're a nurse,' Doctor Mortimer said. 'Did you dress the wound?'

'Yes, that's right.' Rebecca nodded.

'And what happened? Do you know?'

'I've told you what happened,' drawled Piers, from the bed. 'For God's sake, man, I'm not dying. I've cut my shoulder, that's all.'

Paul and Sheila came to the door, standing looking in curiously, and Piers compressed his lips angrily. 'Go away, all of you!' he snapped fiercely. 'If I must have a doctor, I don't need a gaggle of sightseers!'

Paul flushed. 'I'm training to be a doctor, Father, and Sheila is a nurse!'

'Please!' That was Doctor Mortimer. 'This young lady can assist me. I'll speak to you when I come down.'

With an angry exclamation, Paul slammed the door behind them, and Piers turned to Rebecca. 'She can go, too,' he muttered grimly. 'I don't need a nurse.'

Doctor Mortimer ignored him. 'Hand me my bag, would you?' he requested Rebecca, and smiled as she complied. 'Take no notice of him,' he advised, noticing Rebecca's tense expression. 'Piers is not a man to take kindly to dependence upon anybody.'

Piers raised his eyes heavenward, but Rebecca felt slightly relieved. Obviously the doctor was not at all perturbed by his attitude.

Even so, she knew Piers hated her to see him gritting his teeth as the doctor applied a local anaesthetic to the wound before stitching it. It took twelve stitches and afterwards he was given an injection for tetanus before the doctor was satisfied that he had done all that could be done. Piers swung his legs to the ground and sat up, but Rebecca could tell from the pallor of his face that he was not completely recovered, and Doctor Mortimer put a hand on his uninjured shoulder firmly.

'You must rest,' he insisted, frowning. 'You've lost a lot of blood and if you behave stupidly you'll land yourself in hospital.'

Piers shook off his hand and stood up, swaying a little. 'You're an old woman, Mortimer!' he retorted impatiently. 'Nothing has ever prevented me from getting around and nothing ever will.'

'Let us hope not.' Doctor Mortimer was dry. 'Do you intend going back downstairs?'

'Of course.'

Mortimer shrugged. 'You'll collapse again, I warn you.'

Piers pressed his lips together, but there was exasperation now in his gaze. 'You're not serious,' he exclaimed.

'Aren't I?' Doctor Mortimer regarded him wryly.

'*Diabolique!*' Piers glanced down at the neat strapping of his wound. 'Are you telling me I am an invalid, Mortimer?'

'No.' Doctor Mortimer shook his head. 'I'm just

telling you you've got to take it easy for a couple of days. If I were you, I'd go to bed now.'

'We were playing bridge,' Piers exclaimed.

Doctor Mortimer shrugged again. 'Don't let me keep you from your game!'

Piers raked his good hand through his thick hair and glared at Rebecca as though blaming her for everything. 'All right—all right,' he said shortly. 'I'll take your advice.' He walked slowly towards the door, and then looked back at her. 'I will see you tomorrow.' His words brooked no argument and Rebecca said nothing.

After he had gone, Doctor Mortimer looked resignedly at Rebecca. 'Will you be here tomorrow?' he asked anxiously.

Rebecca bit her lip. 'To begin with. But Paul and I go back to London tomorrow.'

'I see.' Doctor Mortimer gnawed at his lip. 'I don't like the look of that cut, do you?'

'What do you mean?'

Mortimer shook his head. 'The lorry that he was pushing: do you know what it carried?'

Rebecca frowned. 'I'm afraid not. I don't even remember what the name was on the side of it. Harman would know.'

Mortimer nodded. 'Well, we'll see. Your immediate cleansing of it with an antiseptic may have avoided any poisoning, but I'll come back tomorrow anyway. I'd have liked to know you were here to keep an eye on it.'

Rebecca ran her tongue over her upper lip. 'Miss— Miss Stephens is a nurse, you know.'

'Adele's companion?'

'Yes.'

Mortimer put his equipment back into his bag and closed it with a snap. 'I don't care for that young woman. If you ask me, she's only here for one reason. She has an eye to the main chance.'

Rebecca felt the familiar coldness invade her stomach. 'What do you mean?'

'It's obvious, isn't it? She turned up here just after Jennifer's death, and whenever Piers is around she's more concerned with him than with her patient. At least, that's what I've observed when I've visited Adele.'

'I see.' Rebecca swallowed hard. 'Even so—she would be of some help . . .'

Mortimer smiled for the first time. 'I've told you, I'll come back myself, until I'm sure it's okay.' He lifted his bag. 'Shall we go down?'

After Doctor Mortimer had gone, Rebecca had to enter the lounge again to confront the others. She would have liked to have avoided this, to have gone straight to bed herself, but of course that was impossible. Besides, Mrs, Gillean was in the process of remaking her bed, taking away the bloodied sheets and pillowcases and replacing them with clean ones. Piers had gone to his own room and Gillean had assisted him to bed, and Paul had already spoken to his father.

But now it was her turn to be questioned, and she hoped she could remain as composed as she outwardly appeared. Adele, as usual, was first to attack.

'Well, miss,' she said bleakly, 'we're waiting for an explanation. Exactly what did you hope to achieve by keeping what was going on from us? A chance to win favour with my brother-in-law?'

Rebecca sank down weakly into an armchair, sure her legs would no longer support her. 'Not—not at all,' she stammered awkwardly, hardly daring to look at Paul. 'It was simply that everything happened so quickly——'

Paul lit a cigarette, inhaling deeply. 'Telling us wouldn't have taken a moment,' he said. 'And before we go any further, I'd like to know how it happened.'

'I've told you. The lorry was splintered metal. Your father tore his shoulder on the metal.' Rebecca stared at him.

Paul studied the **tip** of his cigarette. 'And I suppose you thought here was another chance to shine in his eyes.'

Rebecca's expression was mortified. 'Paul!' she exclaimed.

Paul had the grace to look shamefaced. 'Well...' he said, defensively. 'It's pretty obvious it was something like that. I'd be interested to know exactly how well you knew my father in Fiji.'

Rebecca heaved a sigh, unable to prevent the embarrassment that showed on her face. She looked angrily at Adele and saw her smug expression, and wondered what she had been saying while she was upstairs. Feeling as though nothing would hurt her after this, she said: 'Why don't you ask your aunt?'

Tom Bryant stepped forward. He had been leaning against the cabinet in the corner and she had scarcely noticed him, but now he said: 'Come on, Paul, stop this stupidity. I think Rebecca acted in your father's best interests, and as Doctor Mortimer has told us he put twelve stitches into your father's arm, I hardly think you should complain because you weren't consulted before the doctor was called. Heavens, man, you should be thankful it was not more serious!'

Paul looked a trifle shamefaced. 'It's all right you talking like that, Tom——'

'Oh, stop it!' Tom seemed to be losing his patience. 'What happened, after all? Why should you have been told at once? What could you have done that Rebecca couldn't do just as adequately?'

'Paul is Piers' son,' interrupted Adele sharply.

'So what?'

Adele lifted her shoulders a trifle nervously. 'So you're championing Rebecca, too, are you, Tom?'

Tom gave her an eloquent stare. 'Well, as there are three of you, I think that's only fair, don't you?' he observed sardonically.

Adele flushed. 'Oh, well, leave it, leave it! It's over and there's nothing we can do about it now.' She looked fully at Rebecca. 'You'll be leaving tomorrow?'

Rebecca got to her feet. 'I'd leave tonight if I could,' she said tautly, and left the room before any of them could say anything else.

Outside, in the hall, she leaned against the wall weakly. She was a fool to allow anything Adele said to upset her, but it did. And what Doctor Mortimer had said hurt her, too. It seemed that all the St. Clair family could do was hurt her.

She walked slowly across the hall and heard a door close behind her. Glancing round swiftly, she expected to see Paul, but instead she saw Tom Bryant. She felt relieved. At least Tom believed that what she had done was right.

'Come into the library,' he said. 'You're too upset to go to bed. We can have a drink together. That will help.'

Rebecca hesitated, and then smiled. 'All right. Thanks.'

While Tom prepared their drinks, Rebecca tidied away the records she and Paul had been playing earlier. Then they sat in opposite armchairs and Rebecca sipped the long drink Tom had given her. It was a mixture of lime and lemon and laced with vodka, and it was quite delicious.

'That's better, isn't it?' said Tom, smiling, and Rebecca nodded. 'Much,' she agreed.

'Tell me,' Tom frowned, 'exactly what is your relationship to Paul?'

Rebecca coloured. 'We don't have a—relationship, as such. We're friends, that's all.'

'I see. And of course Paul didn't know you knew his family.'

'No.'

Tom nodded thoughtfully. 'I gather you and Adele don't get on.'

Rebecca half smiled. 'That's the understatement of the year.'

Tom shrugged. 'She's not an easy person to get on with. She's had too much adversity in her life to cope with it sensibly. She had a grudge against life, and against her family, and against anyone who dares to challenge her, I suppose.'

'I used to pity her,' said Rebecca slowly. 'But she doesn't want pity. At least—not from me.'

'No, she never did. I guess that's why she's so embittered. It's gnawed into her soul. Maybe if she'd got rid of some of that bitterness in a normal healthy way, she would have been a different person. But she never could.' He sighed, swirling the liquid round in his glass. 'She's never forgiven Piers for marrying Jennifer, you know. Just as she never forgave Jennifer, although that didn't bother her. The St. Clouds as a family are alike in the respect that they care only for themselves.'

Rebecca frowned. 'Why are you telling me all this?'

Tom shrugged. 'I got the feeling you were interested.'

'I was. I *am!*' Rebecca bit her lip. 'But it's really nothing to do with me, is it?'

'Isn't it?'

'What do you mean?'

Tom swallowed some of his whisky, savouring it for a moment. 'Well, I remember Piers three years ago. When he came back from his exploratory trip to the Yasawas!'

Rebecca's fingers tightened round her glass. 'Oh!'

'Yes.' Tom leant forward, resting his elbows on his knees. 'He—well, something happened out there. I never did find out what, but tonight—when he saw you in the hall——' He lay back in his chair. 'It all came back to me.'

Rebecca bent her head, trembling a little. 'I see.'

Tom gave an involuntary lift of his shoulders. 'If it's any consolation to you now, you must have dealt him a pretty low blow out there.' He shook his head. 'For months he was hell to work with. God knows what he was like to live with!'

Rebecca looked up at him tremulously. 'And he was married, too, wasn't he?'

Tom grimaced. 'Married? Well, I guess you could call it that. But Jennifer was no wife, if that's what you really mean.'

Rebecca rose to her feet, unable to sit still and listen to him. 'It's nothing to do with me,' she said tautly. 'How—how long have you worked with—with Paul's father?'

Tom uttered an exclamation, and then sighed. 'I don't know. Twenty years, I guess. What does it matter?' He drew out his cigarettes, but she refused when he offered them to her. Putting one between his lips, he lit it carefully, and then went to get himself another drink.

Rebecca moved about the room restlessly, fingering the leatherbound volumes that lined the shelves. There were many first additions and it seemed obvious that like the jade these books had been collected over many decades. Tom went back to his chair and watched her with narrowed eyes. Finally he said: 'Did Adele tell you about her sister?'

Rebecca turned slowly, fingering her glass. 'She told me she was in love with Piers herself and that Jennifer took him away from her.'

Tom nodded. 'I see. And you believed that?'

Rebecca sighed. 'Wasn't it the truth?'

'Of course not. Could you see Piers and Adele together?'

Rebecca shrugged. 'I don't know. I imagine Adele was more active when she was younger.'

'She was. But never to the extent of having boy-friends. That was why she hated her sisters. They were always in and out of the house with different men. I guess it was hard for her, and she couldn't take it.'

144

Rebecca shook her head. 'Well, anyway, does it matter? If Adele likes to think she once attracted Piers, does it matter?'

'It does if what she's told you about him is a pack of lies.'

Rebecca clenched her fists. 'Look, Tom,' she said, rather unsteadily, 'whatever happened between me and Piers in Fiji is long over. I was just a—a diversion. One of many in his lifetime, I suppose.'

'Do you really believe that?' Tom frowned. 'Piers has his faults, I know, but he's no animal!'

Rebecca sipped her drink slowly. 'Tom,' she said carefully, 'you're his friend, his good friend obviously. But don't ask me to believe that a man who is willing to have an affair with another woman when he already has a wife at home is to be trusted!'

Tom drew impatiently on his cigarette. 'Don't condemn him too quickly. You obviously have no idea what went on.'

Rebecca gave an involuntary gesture. 'Well, Jennifer had his child, didn't she?' Then she coloured. She was confiding in this man as she had never confided in anyone ever before. But he was so easy to talk with—to share her anxieties with.

Tom sighed. 'Paul is Piers' son, yes. He's never denied it.'

Rebecca moved restlessly. 'You see!' She pressed her lips together. 'Besides, when he was in Fiji he told me he lived outside Paris, and now today I find that he bought this house fifteen years ago. Everything he said was just lies!'

Tom leant forward. 'Piers bought this house for Jennifer.'

Rebecca pressed her hand to her stomach. 'What do you mean?'

'I'll explain.' Tom held her gaze. 'Piers owns four houses. Apart from *Sans-Souci* and the Paris house, he has a villa in the south of France and a house in

145

Jamaica. Jennifer used his houses, yes, but she never shared them with him. They were separated. Do you understand? It's the nearest their church will go to a divorce.'

Rebecca digested this incredulously. If only she had known, but she hadn't. Tom looked angry. 'There's more. Jennifer was purely a bitch! She liked men. Do I make myself clear? And Piers couldn't take it! He despised her, and she sought her pleasures elsewhere.'

'Oh, no!' Rebecca felt revolted.

'Yes. Having Paul nearly killed her, but he was the one redeeming factor of their marriage, the one reason why Piers didn't cut her off without a penny. I don't suppose Paul has any idea of the kind of life his father was forced to lead when his mother was alive. Paul was away—at boarding school—at university. It was all concealed from him. His father's work took him away a lot, and I suppose Paul accepted that his parents were not as happy as they might have been, but that was all. Jennifer, in her way, avoided being too— blatant, while he was around. That was the one condition Piers placed on their artificial relationship. But no one can deny it was a blessed release for him when she died.'

Rebecca stood staring at him. 'How—how did she die?'

'She contracted an incurable disease. The St. Clouds are not a healthy family, and quite honestly I can't confess a regret I didn't feel.'

Rebecca passed a hand over her forehead. 'I suppose whenever I thought about it, Paul's presence got in the way.'

Tom bent his head. 'Piers was only nineteen when he married Jennifer. She was several years older. He's paid for his adolescent irresponsibility, don't you think?'

'Adele made everything sound so different . . .'

'She would. She's a twisted woman. The whole family were twisted, if you ask me. Denise—Jennifer's younger sister—committed suicide when she was twenty-five.'

'That's a terrible story,' said Rebecca, shaking her head. 'Adele told me nothing like that. She made it sound—well—as though Jennifer was the innocent party.'

'I can imagine,' muttered Tom grimly. 'Well, are you going to tell Piers?'

'Tell Piers? Tell him what?'

'That you know the truth now.'

Rebecca drew her brows together. 'I—I couldn't do that. Besides, he—he's not interested in me.' She flushed. 'In what I think.'

Tom lay back in his chair. 'He has no wife now,' he remarked quietly.

Rebecca finished her drink and turned the empty glass between her palms. 'You don't imagine—after all this time——' She swallowed hard. 'I—I think you're presuming too much ...'

Tom shrugged. 'Maybe I am. But wouldn't you like to find out? Or are you really involved with Paul?'

'No! Oh, no, not Paul. He's—well, he's too young. Besides, I could never——' She broke off, feeling slightly sick. Glancing at her watch, she gave an exclamation: 'Do you realise it's almost midnight? We ought to go to bed.'

Tom smiled slowly. 'That's a rather tantalising suggestion,' he murmured lazily. 'Do you know, I'm beginning to understand why Piers wanted you ...'

CHAPTER FIVE

THE following morning Rebecca was awake early, before the first faint fingers of dawn pushed their way through her curtains. She slid out of bed and went to the window, peering out curiously. In the grey gloom she could see that the fog still persisted, although it was much less dense than the night before. She glanced at her watch and saw that it was only a little after seven and there seemed no sounds from anywhere to indicate that anyone else was awake. She washed in the bathroom and then dressed and did her hair, taking her time and wondering whether she dared go downstairs.

Eventually she decided she must do something and she went out of her room on to the landing and through the door into the main gallery. Leaning over the balustrade, she could see the hall below where a young girl was busily cleaning out the stucco-flanked fireplace. Glad that someone else was about, Rebecca went downstairs and as she reached the bottom the maid looked up and saw her.

'Heavens, miss,' she exclaimed in a rough country brogue, 'you startled me!'

Rebecca smiled apologetically. 'I'm sorry. Who are you?'

'I'm Elizabeth, miss. I help Mrs. Gillean.'

Rebecca nodded. 'I see. Well, Elizabeth, perhaps you could help me. Do you know what time breakfast is usually served?'

Elizabeth got to her feet, wiping her hands clean on an old piece of rag. 'Mrs. Gillean doesn't usually serve breakfast, miss. Apart from when Mr. Piers is at home, that is, and then only for him. Miss Adele and Nurse Stephens have theirs together in Miss Adele's suite, and when Mr. Paul is here he doesn't often bother. He prefers to sleep on, I think.'

A ripple of anticipation ran over Rebecca as the maid mentioned Piers, and she quelled it as she said: 'And is—your employer up this morning?'

The maid shook her head vigorously. 'Oh, no, miss. Cook said he was having a tray today. Besides, it's only a little after eight, miss. Mr. Piers doesn't usually get up much before nine.'

'Oh.' Rebecca sighed. Then she said: 'Tell me, where is the cook?'

'Mrs. Gillean, miss? She's in the kitchen. Do you want to see her?'

'Well—yes, all right. Will you show me where to go?'

'Yes, miss. It's just through there—see?'

Rebecca followed the maid's instructions and passed through a baize door which led down a passage to the huge kitchens. She could tell where the kitchen was from the delicious smell that emanated from it, and when she pushed open the door she found Mrs. Gillean busy at the stove frying bacon and sausages. The older woman looked up in surprise as Rebecca came in, and said:

'Oh, Miss—Miss Lindsay, isn't it? Is something wrong?'

'No, nothing, thank you, Mrs. Gillean. I—er—I wondered if I could possibly take up Mr.—Mr. Piers' tray?'

Mrs. Gillean could not have looked more surprised and she coloured hotly, her rosy cheeks brilliant. 'Well —er—I—er—I don't see why not,' she finished awkwardly. 'Er—you mean right now?'

'If that's possible. Is this for him?' Rebecca indicated the bacon and sausages in the pan.

'Bless you, no, miss. Mr. Piers doesn't like anything like that for his breakfast. He likes some of these.' She bent and opened an oven door and drew out a tray of golden brown rolls, newly baked and smelling deliciously.

'Of course.' Rebecca smiled ruefully. 'I should have guessed. Look, you get on with what you're doing, and I'll do this. I used to be Miss Adele's nurse, so I'm used to preparing breakfast trays.'

Mrs. Gillean extracted a tray from a rack on the wall and shook her head firmly. 'Oh, no, miss, if you don't mind. I'll do it myself. I always prepare Mr. Piers' tray myself, even when I have help. It's only right that I should.'

'You know best.' Rebecca stood aside and watched Mrs. Gillean take a sparkling white linen cloth from a drawer and lay it on the tray. Then she went to the stove and put several of the hot rolls into a serviette-lined basket and put it on the tray as well. To go with the rolls there was a dish of curls of butter, a small jar of honey, and a tub of marmalade. Finally Mrs. Gillean added a jug of steaming aromatic continental coffee. 'There you are, miss,' she said. 'But what about your breakfast? What do you like?'

Rebecca shrugged. 'I'm never hungry in the mornings,' she temporised. 'I'll have some coffee when I get back.'

'Very good, miss.' Mrs. Gillean folded her arms.

Rebecca smiled and lifted the tray. Now came the most difficult moment, she thought.

'Er—could you tell me which room is Mr. Piers'?' she asked, walking to the door.

Mrs. Gillean was clearly surprised now, but she hid it admirably. Rebecca felt sure she had decided they had shared the same room.

Piers' room was down a corridor off the main gallery, but with Mrs. Gillean's instructions Rebecca found it easily and knocked gently at the door. There was no reply, and balancing the tray with one hand she turned the handle and entered the room, closing the door behind her.

Piers was still asleep, his face still a little pale from his ordeal of the night before, and Rebecca put down the tray before going to the windows and drawing back the heavy plum-coloured drapes. Now she could see that the room was austerely furnished in dark shades and even the carpet underfoot had none of the softness and depth of her own. Piers in sleep looked younger and strangely vulnerable and her heart rose up in her throat achingly. There was no doubt in her mind now. She loved him and she always had.

The pale light from the windows was disturbing him, and he moved restlessly before opening his eyes. When he saw Rebecca he stared at her disbelievingly. 'Rebecca,' he said questioningly. Then, as awareness came to him: 'Rebecca! What in hell are you doing here?'

Rebecca moved towards the bed, noticing how white the bandage on his arm looked compared to the brownness of his skin. It was the first time, apart from when she was working, that she had seen a man in bed, and awareness of him was like a warmth throughout her body.

'Hello, Piers,' she said, folding her hands behind her back. 'I—I brought your breakfast. How—how do you feel this morning?'

Piers levered himself up on one elbow, the covers falling to his waist. He obviously wore no pyjama jacket. 'Why have you come?' he snapped coldly. 'I don't need any more professional advice from you.'

Rebecca twisted one finger painfully. 'I didn't come to give you professional advice,' she said uneasily. 'I—well, I wanted to talk to you.'

Piers raked a hand through his tousled hair. 'Go on then, talk!' he muttered, wincing as he jarred the dressing on his arm.

'Oh, Piers, you're not making it very easy for me!' Rebecca pressed her lips together. 'I—I just wanted to—to tell you—that—that—I know about—about

151

Jennifer.'

Piers' dark eyes narrowed to slits. 'Indeed.' His tone was bitter.

'Yes. I—Adele told me you—you were going to marry her but you deserted her for Jennifer—and then—and then——'

'Silence!' Piers glared at her furiously. 'Do you think I care what Adele told you? I told you at the time that I had no interest in my sister-in-law's estimation of me!'

'But—don't you see—I believed her!'

'Yes, you did.' His expression was contemptuous. 'You believed her—and you would not listen to me!'

'But——'

'But nothing.' Piers rubbed one hand over the bandage as though it pained him. 'You believed her because that is what you wanted to believe.'

'*No!*' The word was torn from her.

'But yes. You were—you *are*—such a timid creature.' His tone was cruelly derisive. 'You are afraid to exhibit any emotion! You are confined by your own narrow-minded inhibitions! You are afraid to love without security!' He gave a scornful laugh. 'And you come here now to tell me that suddenly you understand—that suddenly you regret what you said—what you did! What do you expect from me, I wonder? What kind of reaction am I supposed to make? Do I say—Rebecca, all is forgiven? Do I say—Rebecca, you have made me very happy? Do I say—Rebecca, I am free now, will you marry me? *Non!*'

He slid abruptly out of bed and Rebecca turned tremblingly away, for as he reached for the silk dressing gown which lay at the foot of his bed she saw that he slept without any garment whatsoever.

'You see!' he muttered savagely in her ear, 'you turn away your eyes because you are afraid. And believe me,' his voice deepened, 'you have every reason to be so!'

Rebecca pressed her hands together in front of her. She should have known it was useless to come here, to attempt to explain to this embittered stranger that she had been hopelessly unaware that she was merely a pawn in the hands of an unscrupulous woman; vulnerable because she had no confidence in her own ability to attract him. Maybe he was right, maybe she had wanted to believe Adele because the alternative had offered too precarious an enchantment . . .

On unsteady legs she moved to the door, but he was there before her, leaning back against it, preventing her escape from this humiliation. 'One moment,' he said harshly, 'I want you to tell me something before I let you go. Do you intend to go on seeing my son?'

Rebecca linked and unlinked her fingers. 'As we work in the same building, it would be impossible not——'

'Damn you, that is not what I meant, and you know it!' His eyes glittered angrily. 'Does he make love to you?'

'*No!*' The word was torn from her. 'Of course not.'

Piers' eyes narrowed. 'Why—*of course not*? You are —you always were—a most desirable woman.' He moved slowly but deliberately towards her. 'How many men, I wonder, have made love to you since I——'

Rebecca's fingers stung across his cheek with angry resentment. 'How—how dare you?' she cried chokingly.

Piers did not seem to notice her outburst. His hard fingers closed over her shoulders, drawing her resistingly towards him, close against the lean, hard **streng**th of his body. She could feel the hardness of his muscles through the thin dressing gown and she struggled to free herself desperately. But her movements only stimulated him more and he bent his head and put his mouth to hers, parting her lips with such determined expertise that for a few moments she lost coherent thought and clung to him. It was incredible to believe that it was three years since he had held her in his arms, for it could have been yesterday and all the agony in between was as nothing when he bruised her neck and shoulders with ruthless passion. Rebecca was on fire for him, but the mounting urgency of his lovemaking sent warning spears of pain along her veins, for she knew that this time he did not intend to draw back . . .

With a superhuman effort, she dragged herself away from him, realising as she did so that she must have hurt his injured arm. But all she could think of was the need to get away from him before the warmth of his skin beneath her fingers seduced her to abandon all attempts at escape, and she would submit to his undoubted masculinity.

She wrenched open the door, not daring to look back at him, and ran wildly down the corridor to the gallery. Only there did she halt and try to assume some degree of composure, although her hair was a tumbled mass about her shoulders and the buttons of her jacket were undone.

She went to her bedroom, closing the door and leaning back against it weakly. She had been a fool to go to him, but an even bigger fool allowing him to touch her. How he must despise her to treat her so. If only they were not so isolated here, she would walk out of the house now and make her own way back to London.

Eventually she calmed herself. It was after ten now and time she was seeking Paul to find out what he intended to do. She hoped and prayed he would agree to leave before lunch. She did not think she could bear to encounter Piers again.

Downstairs she found Paul already waiting for her. 'Have you had breakfast?' he asked, eyeing her dourly.

Rebecca bit her lip. 'No, but I don't want anything. Are—are you ready to leave?'

'*I* am,' asserted Paul insinuatingly. 'Are you?'

'Is there any reason why I should not be?'

Paul shrugged. 'I thought you might insist on seeing my father before you leave.'

Rebecca's cheek's burned. 'Oh, no! No,' she denied uncomfortably. 'Have—have you seen him?'

'Yes, I've seen him,' Paul nodded.

Rebecca twisted the strap of her handbag. 'How—how is he?'

Paul shrugged. 'He has some pain with his shoulder. He is going to have Sheila dress it for him.'

A knife-like pain tore through Rebecca's stomach. 'Oh—oh, is he?'

Paul watched her carefully. 'Yes. Why not? She's a very competent nurse. You behave as though he was your patient.'

'I don't.' Rebecca turned away. 'Shall we go?'

'Don't you want to see Sheila—and my aunt—to say goodbye?'

Rebecca pressed her lips together mutinously. 'No.'

Paul shrugged and rose from the armchair where he had been lounging with negligent grace. 'All right. The car's outside.'

Rebecca looked back once as Paul's car moved smoothly down the drive, but as when she arrived the windows seemed blank and empty and an awful sense of desolation enveloped her. She glanced at Paul and found him staring broodingly ahead through the windscreen. The fog was practically gone and a weak sun was trying to push through the low-hanging clouds. But Paul's face registered only an inner sulkiness, and Rebecca sighed heavily. It was going to be a long journey back to London.

They drove through the village, taking the Harpenden road as they had done on their outward journey yesterday. But they did not stop there, and drove on towards the outer suburbs of London, stopping for lunch at a roadhouse on the Slough road. Paul had spoken little since their departure, but after the waiter had taken their order in the restaurant and they had been served with a pre-lunch martini, he said: 'Don't you think you owe me an explanation?'

Rebecca sipped her martini slowly. 'What about?'

Paul glared at her. 'You must know!' he said angrily.

Rebecca shrugged her shoulders exasperatedly. 'From your attitude I should imagine you think you know already,' she remarked.

Paul pressed his fist against the table. 'Aunt Adele only told me what she thought I ought to know.'

Rebecca controlled the impulse to retaliate angrily; she would not give Adele the satisfaction of knowing she had disturbed her again. 'What did she tell you then?' she asked, with assumed complacency.

Paul sighed. 'Oh, Rebecca, it's not true, is it?' He shook his head looking suddenly very young and very vulnerable.

Rebecca sighed. 'I don't know what you've been told.'

Paul flushed. 'She said that—that you and my father were lovers when he was in Fiji.'

Rebecca clenched her fists in her lap. She felt furiously angry. How dared Adele suggest such a thing? How dared she slander both of them in such an outrageous manner? She swallowed hard, trying to contain her resentment. It wasn't Paul's fault that his aunt chose to use her prying against her own brother-in-law. And after all, it might be that Adele really believed they had been lovers ... How twisted her mind must be by so much intrigue.

Now Rebecca looked at Paul and knew she had to tell him the truth. 'No,' she said clearly, 'your father and I were not lovers.' She watched him intently. 'Do you believe me?'

Paul swallowed half his martini and then nodded. 'Yes,' he said, rather jerkily. 'Yes, I believe you.'

'Do you?' Rebecca frowned. 'I wonder.'

'Why do you say that?' Paul looked indignantly at

her. 'I—I've told you, I believe you. I know Aunt Adele—exaggerates sometimes.'

'Exaggerates!' Rebecca lifted her martini and studied it intently. 'Your aunt is a malicious trouble-maker! Believe me, that's the truth.'

Paul looked embarrassed. 'She means no harm——'

'You think not?' Rebecca sounded incredulous. Then she bent her head. 'Anyway, there is something I ought to explain. While your father and I were never lovers, we were—attracted to one another.' She looked up at him candidly. 'Three years ago in Fiji, I mean.'

Paul looked flabbergasted now. 'But—but my father was a married man! Do you mean to tell me that meant nothing to you—to either of you?' His eyes searched hers disbelievingly.

Rebecca coloured now. 'Of course it meant some-thing. Oh, Paul, it's a long story, but in short your aunt—your misunderstood aunt—encouraged us. She chose not to tell me that Piers—that your father—was married.'

Paul hunched his shoulders. 'But my father knew.'

'I know.'

Paul shook his head. 'I never guessed. Oh, I knew my parents didn't get on, of course, but nor did many of the parents of the boys at my school. I guess it's the current trend. It was nothing out of the ordinary. But I never thought—I never dreamt—that my father was unfaithful to her.' He looked up. 'You never knew my mother, of course?'

Rebecca shook her head.

Paul sighed. 'What a situation! No wonder she turned to—to other men.'

'You *knew*!' Rebecca was incredulous.

'Oh, yes. Aunt Adele told me . . .' His voice trailed away and he looked helplessly at her. 'You mean—there's more?'

Rebecca turned away, looking hopelessly round the restaurant. 'Oh, no, nothing more,' she exclaimed.

'Paul, let's change the subject. It's all over now. It was all over three years ago. Your mother's dead, your father's alive. Let's just leave it at that, shall we?'

Paul stared down at the plate in front of him. 'I can't leave it,' he muttered grimly. 'Who told you anyway?'

Rebecca shrugged. 'Tom. Tom Bryant.'

'I see.' Paul sighed, and then to Rebecca's relief the waiter arrived with their first course and conversation waned.

It was late in the afternoon when they arrived back at Rebecca's apartment and she slid out eagerly saying: 'I won't invite you in, Paul. I—I'm going to have a lazy evening.'

Paul nodded miserably. 'Will I see you tomorrow?'

Rebecca moved awkwardly. 'Oh, I don't think so, Paul——'

'Please.'

She shook her head helplessly and then gave in. 'All right,' she agreed. 'You can come round for a drink in the evening if you like.'

Paul's expression lightened. 'Thanks. Be seeing you!'

Rebecca nodded and closed the door and watched as he drove away. Then she went into the apartment and locked her door with relief. At last she was in her own home and able to lick her wounds in private.

Three days later she went down with influenza.

Ever since her return from *Sans-Souci* she had felt under the weather, but she had put that down to the obvious depression which had engulfed her on her return. However, on Tuesday evening it became patently obvious that something more physical was wrong.

She had finished work at the usual time and gone back to the apartment to make her evening meal. Paul was coming round later, she had put him off the previous evening, but on Tuesday she could think of no feasible excuse. She felt, therefore, that it was retribution that she should have contracted the chill as she did and found herself unable to ring Paul to make that excuse. He would be sure to imagine she was making it up and it was far better that he should come and see for himself.

Even so she had not expected to feel so ill on her return home and far from making herself a meal, she put on the electric fire and after changing into slacks and a chunky sweater, she huddled over it, trying to keep warm. But whatever she did, she shivered, and she knew she ought to go to bed.

Paul arrived soon after nine. Rebecca let him in and he saw at once from her streaming eyes and puffy cheeks that something was wrong.

'Heavens!' he exclaimed, 'you ought to be in bed, don't you know that?'

Rebecca nodded chokily. 'Yes,' she said nasally. 'But you were coming and I didn't like to put you off again.'

Paul smiled gently at her. 'I see. Well,' he put a professional hand to her forehead, 'I would suggest you get into bed right away and I'll give old Manley a ring and see if he can come over and look at you.'

'Oh, no!' Rebecca was horrified at this suggestion. 'It's only a cold, Paul. Nothing serious. But I agree with you, I ought to be in bed. Would you mind?'

'Would I mind what?'

'Going, of course.'

Paul put an arm about her shoulders comfortingly, 'Rebecca, I have no ulterior motives for staying, believe me, but I'd prefer to see you into bed before I leave. Where's the kitchen? I'll get you a hot water bottle and a warm drink. Do you have any aspirins?'

Rebecca gave him an exasperated smile. 'Honestly, Paul, I can manage. Don't try to practise your bedside manner on me. Besides, I have an electric blanket and an electric kettle, and I can easily plug them both in while I get undressed. It's kind of you to offer, but no——'

Paul heaved a sigh. 'You don't trust me, do you?'

Rebecca spread her hands. 'Of course I do. In any case, no one could have designs on me tonight. I look ghastly.'

Paul hesitated a moment longer and then with a dejected shrug he walked to the door. 'All right, all right, I'll go. But I'll be back tomorrow. Don't you dare to get up if you're no better in the morning.'

'No—no, all right, thank you, Doctor—Victor.' Rebecca bit her lip. Suddenly her words had brought everything back to her and to Paul obviously from the distressed look on his face.

'I'll go,' he said, compressing his lips resignedly, and Rebecca saw him out of the door.

On Wednesday morning her cold was much worse and she was hoarse and had difficulty in breathing. It seemed obvious that she had contracted this on that foggy Saturday evening and she tossed restlessly in her bed before getting up weakly to ring the hospital.

Matron was very understanding and insisted on sending one of the doctors over to look at her. Doctor Manley was a middle-aged man with children of his own, and he looked at Rebecca over his spectacles rather chidingly.

'It's these short skirts you girls wear!' he observed dryly. 'Little wonder you all catch colds. I'm surprised you don't catch pneumonia! Tell me, do you have anyone here to look after you?'

Rebecca sighed, sniffing miserably. She felt terrible and she wished he would just go away and leave her in peace. 'No,' she said, breathily. 'But I'm all right. I can manage.'

Dr. Manley frowned. 'How? How can you manage? Who will look after you? Who will get you your medicine when you need it? Provide you with hot drinks—

all the little things you need. Meals, for example.'

'I'm not hungry.' Rebecca drew the covers round her chin.

'No, maybe not at the moment. But you will be.'

'Then I'll get up . . .'

Dr. Manley shook his head. 'Can't have one of the nursing sisters taking unnecessary risks with her health,' he intoned grimly. 'Look, I'll have a word with Matron and see if we can't get you into a bed in the isolation wing, eh?'

'Oh, no.' Rebecca lifted her swollen lids. 'I tell you, I'll be all right.'

But by the end of that dreadful day it became obvious that she most definitely was not all right, and that this was no simple cold she had contracted. She felt sick and trembling, aching in every limb, with a hammering pain in her temples that made her dizzy every time she tried to lift her head from the pillow. Dr. Manley took charge as the competent doctor he was, and late in the evening she was installed in a bed in the wing usually reserved for patients with infectious diseases. By this time Rebecca had to admit to herself that it was a relief to pass her responsibilities on to someone else.

For ten days her life seemed to hang in the balance. The 'flu had deteriorated into pneumonia as Dr. Manley had been afraid it might, and only drugs kept her alive. Rebecca knew little of what went on. She slept a lot in between attacks of breathlessness and she seemed to drink gallons of liquid. The faces who came and went so frequently in her room meant little to her, and only her own misery seemed to penetrate her consciousness.

Then one morning she awoke to find the fever had left her and she was not bathed in sweat as she usually was. When she lifted her head to look about her the pain had gone, too, and there was a blessed lightness about her body.

She managed to eat a little that day and in consequence felt a little stronger, but when she saw her reflection in the mirror in the bathroom she was horrified at the change in herself. The flesh seemed to have fallen off her body and her face seemed thin and pallid. Could she really have changed so dramatically in such a short time? It was incredible. But Dr. Manley thrust her protestations aside when she tried to tell him of her astonishment, merely assuring her solemnly that she was very lucky to be alive and that she would soon get back her strength and her colour.

After that she improved daily, taking a little more food each mealtime and generally trying to take an interest in her surroundings. Some of the nurses in the hospital with whom she was friendly came to see her and she looked forward to their chatter. It distracted her mind from other problems.

Towards the end of the second week Paul came to see her. He brought her an enormous bunch of roses and her nurse looked at them admiringly. 'Roses in December,' she observed lightly. 'How lucky you are.'

To Rebecca's relief Paul did not mention his own affairs. He talked about her illness and the shock it had given all of them, but kept their conversation in a light vein, and seemed less intense than she remembered.

After he had gone, her nurse came back with the roses in water. 'Aren't they beautiful!' she exclaimed, smiling at Rebecca. 'I didn't know you knew Paul Victor.'

Rebecca sighed. 'Oh, yes. I—er—went out with him a couple of times.'

'Oh, did you?' The girl raised her eyebrows. 'And now?'

'I think it's all over,' said Rebecca, pleating the bedspread carefully. 'Why?'

The young nurse chuckled. 'Just that he doesn't seem the constant type.'

Rebecca smiled, too. 'We were just friends, you know.'

'Oh, that's all right, then. I happen to know he went out with a friend of mine a couple of nights ago.'

Rebecca raised her eyebrows, amazed at the relief the girl's words had brought to her. Until then she had thought he was too involved to break away. She sighed. Obviously she had too inflated an idea of her own importance. Still, it was a relief to know that she didn't have to feel guilty about him any more. And a relief too to break all threads with the St. Clair family ...

It was four weeks before she was allowed to go home and it was already the middle of December. The days were colder and the flat seemed empty and devoid of human contact when she arrived back. The neighbour from the floor below had taken the trouble to turn on her fire and there was a welcome warmth issuing from the storage radiators. She had obtained some food on her way home and once a pan was simmering on the stove and the kettle was whistling merrily she felt more relaxed. It was silly to feel so low just because she had come home. Heavens, she hadn't wanted to go into hospital, had she? Still, the sooner she got back to work the better.

In the middle of the evening, when she was watching television, the doorbell rang. Rebecca sighed and got up reluctantly. The unaccustomed effort of making her own meal had tired her more than she would have thought possible and she hoped if this was her neighbour from downstairs she would not stay long.

However, when she opened the door, she found a strange man on the threshold.

Rebecca was taken aback and stood holding the door rather nervously, wondering who he could be and whether he knew she was alone here. All of a sudden she hoped the neighbour from downstairs would appear.

'Miss Lindsay?' the man asked. He was tall and thin and middle-aged, and he wore horn-rimmed spectacles. 'Miss Rebecca Lindsay?'

'Y-yes,' agreed Rebecca reluctantly. 'Who—who are you?'

'My card, Miss Lindsay,' the man held out a narrow strip of cardboard. 'Mr St. Clair sent me . . .'

'Mr. St.—Clair!' Rebecca looked down at the card curiously. It said simply: *Daniel F. Halliday: Private Investigator.*

She looked up at the man in astonishment and then her bewilderment turned to resentment and anger. So he was having her investigated! He had asked her at *Sans-Souci* if she knew who Halliday was, and now she did. She stared at the man through eyes suddenly glazed with tears. How dared he? How dared he have her investigated like some common creature who he thought was unfit to associate with his son!

'Get out!' she cried blindly. 'Go away! I don't want to speak to you! I *won't* speak to you.'

She threw the slip of cardboard in his face and made to slam the door.

'Miss Lindsay—wait—you don't understand——'

'Oh, yes, I do. Go away! Go away before I call the police and have you ejected!'

With a forceful thrust she slammed the door in his face and secured the bolt and chain before turning the key in the lock. She heard him hammering on her door, begging her to open it, telling her that he had something to tell her, something urgent, but she would not listen. Instead, she left the door and walked into the living room, turning up the television so that he would be bound to hear it and realise that whatever he was trying to say he was wasting his time.

Eventually he went away and she turned the television down again, but she found she was trembling. She felt resentful and unhappy. How could Piers do this to her? What was he afraid of? What secrets did he hope to unearth? Surely he knew that Paul was almost bound to tire of being involved with a woman who could give him so little? Or didn't he know that? She didn't know any more ...

She hunched her shoulders and tried to re-interest herself in the play she had been watching on the television, but thoughts plagued her head and she couldn't understand what was going on any more. If Piers had gone so far as to put a private investigator on to her then he must know everything about her by this time. He must know about Sheila and Peter Feldman, for example, if he had not already been told a garbled version by Adele, for it seemed obvious that Sheila was in the other woman's confidence, and that was something they would find easy to translate into their own terms. Maybe that was another reason why he seemed to despise her so.

She got unsteadily to her feet. If she continued to think like this she would drive herself insane. She went out to the kitchen and began to make some coffee. Tomorrow she would go and see Matron and ask her how soon she could get back to the hospital. Only by working and tiring her body to exhaustion could she get any kind of mental relief ...

CHAPTER SIX

But when Rebecca went to see Matron the following day she received another disappointment. Matron was kind and gentle, but she was also firm.

'My dear girl,' she said, resting her elbows on her desk and leaning towards Rebecca, 'you've just recovered from a particularly virulent attack of pneumonia. I could not possibly take you on here again until you have had time to fully recuperate. My best advice to you is wait until the New Year is here, have a break now, and come and see me again towards the end of January.'

Rebecca stared at her incredulously. 'Towards the end of January?' she echoed faintly.

'Yes, at the very earliest. If we were in the height of summer I might suggest you took a month at the sea and then returned to work gradually, but this weather is very bad for you and quite honestly I'm afraid you'd collapse if you put too great a strain on your energies.' She sighed as she saw Rebecca's dejected face. 'My dear girl, I'm not doing this to be unkind. I just want you to be properly well before you return.'

Rebecca came out of Matron's study feeling absolutely shattered. She had pinned all her hopes on getting back into a routine, putting things back into perspective and resuming a normal life. But it seemed even that was to be denied her, for the time being at least, and she had weeks and weeks stretching ahead of her with nothing to do except think . . .

Back at her apartment she gave way to tears. Lying on her bed, staring blindly at her bedroom ceiling, she wondered if she would ever feel normal again.

Annette Fleming came to see her that evening and she was frankly shocked by her friend's appearance.

'Come on, Rebecca,' she exclaimed anxiously. 'Don't be so down-hearted, just because you can't get back to work. Heavens, I should have thought you would appreciate the break. Particularly when the weather's so cold and nobody wants to crawl out of bed these icy mornings.'

Rebecca shrugged miserably. 'But what can I do?' she cried despairingly. 'I have no family like you. No—no boy-friend.'

Annette frowned. 'Well, why don't you do as Matron says and take a holiday? You're not hard up, are you? You could go abroad. It would be exciting.'

Rebecca sat up in her seat and frowned. It was quite an idea when she considered it seriously. And at least, as Annette said, it would take her out of England for a time. In some foreign country she would be just another anonymous tourist . . .

'Where would you go, then?' she asked Annette.

Annette considered for a moment. 'At this time of the year you'd have to go quite a distance to be sure of the sun. North Africa or the Caribbean even. Could your finances stretch so far?'

Rebecca cupped her chin on one hand. 'Why not? I don't go out much. I never seem to spend any money, except on clothes, of course.'

'Lucky you.' Annette stretched her arms above her head lazily. 'Honestly, Rebecca, now you're thinking seriously about it, I feel positively green with envy.'

Rebecca found herself smiling. 'Then it's a pity you can't come, too.'

Annette gave a rueful grimace. 'Unlike you, I do go out a lot and my finances are almost nil. Besides, Barry wouldn't like it.'

Rebecca lay back in her chair, her eyes suddenly thoughtful. The more she thought about it the more desirable the idea became. If she went somewhere far afield, somewhere like the Caribbean for example, there would be little chance of meeting anyone she knew. Momentarily she recalled that Tom Bryant had said that Piers had a house in Jamaica, and she made a mental note not to be tempted to go there...

During the next few days she made definite enquiries about taking a holiday and she renewed her passport. There were so many exciting possibilities to choose from and she spent her evenings poring over travel brochures. Now that she had something with which to occupy her mind it wasn't so difficult to get by and she resumed an interest in herself, having her hair trimmed and styled and buying some new clothes.

Then towards the end of that week a letter came for her. It was from a firm of solicitors in Lincolns Inn advising her that she was one of the beneficiaries under the terms of a last will and testament made by a Miss Adele Margaret St. Cloud...

Rebecca was absolutely stunned by the news. She had never imagined Adele might die so soon, and although she had not liked her, in truth at times she had almost hated her, she would not have wished her dead. It seemed unbelievable that the hysterical tyrant who had caused her so much misery in her life should actually be dead. Although, as Rebecca herself had been told many times by the doctor in Fiji, the attacks she suffered could one day be fatal and she must therefore guard against too much excitement. Rebecca could not deny the faint feeling of compassion which stole over her, even though she knew that Adele would not have thanked her for it.

Reading the letter again, she found it difficult to believe that Adele could have left her anything. After all, she had not liked her, she had tried to hurt her, and on her visit to *Sans-Souci*, that disastrous visit, she had made it plain that she still despised her.

And yet, amazingly, she was summoned to the offices of Messrs. Kitchener, Francis, and Morrison, to hear something to her advantage.

But did she want anything from Adele? Could she take whatever it was Adele had left without being continually reminded of what was past? Or was that Adele's idea? Was her mind distorted to the last to the extent that she was trying to hurt Rebecca after death?

Rebecca paced the flat restlessly. Curiosity was a powerful weapon, and Adele knew what she was doing when she had placed that weapon in Rebecca's hands.

Finally she decided she would have to go to see the solicitors. After all, whatever it was Adele had left her could not be passed on to someone else without her taking a hand in the passing. And as she was hoping to leave England soon anyway, it should be done at once.

She rang the solicitors and made an arrangement to see a Mr. Broome the following morning at eleven. As she stepped out of the taxi outside of the offices, she trembled a little, realising that it was quite possible that one or more members of Adele's family could be here at the same time. But when she was shown into Mr. Broom's office she was relieved to discover that she was his only client at that moment.

He was quite a young man and he explained that although his father had actually been Miss St. Cloud's solicitor he was dealing with this side of it. Rebecca thanked him and then waited patiently for him to go on.

'As you are aware, Miss St. Cloud owned a villa, outside of Suva on the main Fijian island of Viti Levu. I believe at one time you worked there as Miss St. Cloud's nurse, is that correct?'

Rebecca nodded. 'For two years, yes.'

Mr. Broome nodded himself. 'Good.' He consulted the papers on his desk. 'I have here a copy of Miss St. Cloud's last will and testament, and in it she states that she wishes you to have the villa and sufficient funds every year to maintain it.' Ignoring Rebecca's gasp of astonishment, he went on: 'If you should decide to sell the villa, the yearly allowance will naturally cease.' He flicked over another page of the manuscript. 'The money is to be sent to some obscure charity, I believe.'

'You can't be serious!' Rebecca was staring at him incredulously. 'You can't mean she's left the villa—to me!'

Mr. Broome regarded her frowningly. 'Why do you say that, Miss Lindsay? It's here in black and white. I shan't bother you with all the unnecessary details of the preamble, but be assured the villa is yours.'

Rebecca ran a hand over her forehead confusedly. 'But I thought—I mean—she'd lived in England for so long—I assumed the villa had been sold.'

'Oh, no, Miss Lindsay. There is a woman—a Fijian, I believe—looking after it for her.'

'Rosa!' Rebecca said the word almost experimentally. 'It will be Rosa.' She pressed a hand to her throat. 'But—but does she say why? I mean—I just can't believe it.'

Mr. Broome smiled. He was a very self-contained young man and Rebecca couldn't imagine him getting excited about anything. 'My dear Miss Lindsay, as I understand it, Fiji is the other side of the world. Not everyone would want to live there—miles from western civilisation.'

Rebecca compressed her lips. 'Oh, but you're wrong!' she exclaimed. 'It's a marvellous place. Have you ever been to the Melanesian islands, Mr. Broome?'

'I'm afraid not.' Mr. Broome's lips thinned. He turned back to his papers once more. 'I realise you will need time to consider the matter, to think it over, as it were, so I suggest you go away now and come back tomorrow, or the following day, and give me your instructions.'

Rebecca nodded blankly, getting to her feet with nervous haste so that she dropped her gloves and almost her handbag. Fumblingly she picked them up and made her way to the door. Mr. Broome opened it smoothly, and she stepped outside, wondering whether any of his clients aroused him to a more considered awareness of what he was offering them.

In the street she halted, realising that it would be impossible for her to accomplish anything until she had had time to sit down and actually consider the possibilities of what Adele had offered her. It was like some wild dream and she couldn't take it in. Putting aside the fact that Adele had never liked her it still left the incredulous fact that she now owned a villa in Fiji and what was she going to do about it?

There were several things she could do. She could return to the solicitor and tell him she wanted neither the villa nor the money with which to maintain it and have him sell it and send all the money to the obscure charity he had mentioned. Or she could keep the villa, maintain it, and use it whenever she thought fit. Or she could do as Adele had done, so many years before her, and leave England altogether and settle out there. She would need to work, of course, but that wouldn't trouble her, for it seemed obvious that the money Adele was leaving was just to maintain the villa and not herself as well. But she could easily get a post out there, either privately or with a hospital; Doctor Manson would help her, and she would be able to make a whole new life.

Only one thought troubled her and it was a thought she most determinedly thrust down; that of knowing that Piers would be thousands of miles away in England, and there would be no faint chance of ever seeing him again...

But what chance was there anyway? He despised her, he had even had her investigated; if ever she did see him again it would only cause her more humiliation and she didn't think she could stand that.

She hardly slept that night. She wanted to confide in someone, but there was no one she could confide in.

She thought of Paul, and then dismissed the idea. He was making a new life for himself. It was no use her dragging him back into her old one out of a selfish desire to confide in him. There was Annette, of course, but she knew so little of what had gone on that Rebecca could not contemplate confessing her past to her.

So she lay, in solitary indecision, wondering whether she was a fool to consider throwing Adele's money aside to achieve a posthumous revenge. But as the dawn light filtered into her bedroom she was forced to accept that there was nothing she could do to change what was past and she would be a fool to refuse what was being offered. Whatever Adele's motives she could never be really certain what she had intended.

Mr. Broome seemed extremely satisfied with her decision to accept and she told him she intended flying out to Fiji at the end of the following week only three days before Christmas. It seemed fitting somehow that she should be going to spend Christmas in her new home, although she had not entirely decided whether she would live there or not. Maybe it would be possible to compromise, but in any case she needed more time to decide definitely.

She came out of the solicitor's office feeling almost lighthearted. In ten days she would be on her way and she no longer had the prospect of a lonely Christmas at the flat ahead of her ...

Rebecca rolled on to her stomach, digging her fingers deeply into the sand, loving the revitalising heat of the sun on her bare back and shoulders. She had just swum in the warm depths of the Pacific, and now she lay prone on her own beach, soaking up the rays of the sun. Her hair was a wild disorder of gold silk about her and she didn't care. There was no one to see her. Apart from Rosa, of course, and she took little notice of Rebecca's appearance.

It was two days since Rebecca had arrived in Fiji, and tomorrow was Christmas Day. It seemed incredible that London should be having such cold, damp weather when here there was so much warmth and colour. For two days she had done nothing but swim and laze in the sun and already a faint golden tan was covering her pale skin. She was still painfully thin, but she knew that several weeks of Rosa's delicious cooking would put that right. The middle-aged Fijian had been absolutely delighted to see her, and although they had not fully discussed Adele's reasons for leaving Rebecca the villa it would come later. For the present, it was enough to be here, to exchange casual gossip and to know that they understood one another.

Now she glanced up and saw Rosa crossing the sand towards her carrying a white envelope. Pushing herself up on her arms, she sat back on her knees and said: 'What is it, Rosa?'

Rosa halted beside her, handing her the envelope. 'It's a letter, miss. It came just a few minutes ago and I thought you would like to see it.'

Rebecca frowned, taking the envelope and turning it over curiously in her hands. It had been redirected from her London address so that whoever had written to her did not yet know she had left the country. She had given her new address to her neighbour at the flat and obviously it was she who had redirected it.

Rosa smiled and saying something about leaving her oven walked away leaving Rebecca to open the envelope with slightly unsteady fingers. She couldn't imagine who could be writing to her and a faint sense of impending disaster touched her. It was ridiculous to feel this way, she thought impatiently, drawing out the letter she found inside, and yet she was still not immune from the finger of apprehension. Who would want to contact her and not know she had left her flat?

It was not a long letter, and glancing to the end she

found with a prick of unease that Sheila Stephens had written it. Crossing her legs, she began to read and as she did so all her newfound sense of contentment began to disappear . . .

Dear Rebecca, it began. *By the time you read this you will have heard that you have inherited Adele's villa, but as a friend I felt I should inform you that Adele St. Cloud did not leave you anything. On the contrary she died without making any will whatsoever.*

Rebecca's fingers trembled and she had to steady them before she could read on, the writing became so blurred.

In fact, the villa did not belong to her, but to Piers St. Clair. He bought it from her on her return to England and it has remained his ever since. The reason it has been transferred to you is quite simple. For some reason Piers feels guilty about the way he has treated you and consequently he has chosen this way of salving his conscience. Besides, maybe he feels that it is a very satisfactory way of getting you out of the country and therefore out of his, and Paul's, hair. Anyway, as an old friend of yours I thought you deserved to know what you were letting yourself in for by accepting. Sincerely yours, Sheila.

Rebecca thrust the letter aside, and sat for a few minutes just staring blindly out to sea. The sea was at its most beautiful at that hour of the morning, deepening from palest turquoise to richest blue, fringed by the lacy fragility of the coral sand. Along the shoreline palms moved their fronds in the gentle breeze, while their slender trunks provided avenues of shade. The sound of the surf thundering on the reef came to her ears and she thought how unbelievably beautiful it all

174

was. For almost two weeks now she had considered it hers, but suddenly with the advent of this letter it had all been taken away from her. It was no friendly gesture on Sheila's part that had caused her to write that letter. It had been a spiteful attempt to destroy Rebecca's happiness and it had succeeded. Sheila knew as well as anyone else that Rebecca would never find herself able to accept the gift of the villa from Piers St. Clair, whatever his motives, and it had been supposed to arrive before her departure and thus prevent her from ever leaving London. But owing to the irregularity of the postal services, inundated as they were with the Christmas rush, it had been delayed and consequently she had spent all her money coming here needlessly.

She got slowly to her feet and stepped across the turf and entered the villa. Looking about her with newly awakened eyes, she tried to tell herself that it didn't matter, but of course it did. It was the cruellest possible action on Sheila's part and convinced Rebecca finally that the girl had never forgiven her for attracting Peter Feldman. As for Piers St. Clair and his reasons for giving her the villa, she could not possibly understand them. Unless he did, as Sheila intimated, want her out of the way.

After a shower, dressed in cotton pants and a sleeveless blouse, she went into the lounge and flung herself into a chair to read the letter again. When Rosa came in Rebecca handed her the letter, saying: 'Read that, Rosa,' in a thoroughly dejected voice.

Rosa wiped her hands on her apron and then picked up the letter and began to read it silently. When she had finished she looked up, her face showing her puzzlement. 'What does it mean?'

Rebecca slid off her chair. 'It means the villa isn't mine after all. It belongs to Monsieur Piers St. Clair.'

Rosa stared at her disbelievingly. 'You mean—you mean you won't be living here!'

'That's right.' Rebecca compressed her lips to prevent them from trembling. 'I—I shall be going back to London as soon as I can.'

'Oh, Miss Lindsay!' Rosa pressed her hands together at her breast, her black face revealing her disappointment. 'But why? The villa has been given to you. Does it matter by whom?'

Rebecca sighed. 'I'm afraid so. I—I couldn't accept such a gift. Not from—from Monsieur St. Clair.'

Rosa moved her head from side to side in a swaying motion. 'But that's terrible! Tomorrow it's Christmas! You can't mean to leave on Christmas Day!'

Rebecca gathered her thoughts. Of course, she had forgotten. Tomorrow was Christmas Day. She could not leave then. She would have to wait until the Bank Holiday was over. It was ridiculous to feel this sense of relief at the realisation. She had not realised before how much of a retreat the villa had become. To contemplate leaving it was anathema to her.

That night she cried herself to sleep, her pillow soaked with her tears. It was the only time she would cry, she determined, but for the moment the heartbreak could not be denied.

There was a gift for her from Rosa on Christmas morning and when she opened it she found it was a pair of ear-rings made of shells, long and dangling, and thoroughly exotic in design. She had bought a gift for Rosa and the woman was delighted with the blouse she had brought her from England. She insisted on wearing it straight away and to please her Rebecca put on the shell ear-rings, feeling them touch her shoulder as they swung and swayed languidly. They looked rather incongruous with the white bikini which was her only garment, but Rosa was pleased and there was no one else to see them.

They had a light lunch and in the early evening they ate a roast turkey which Rosa had got especially to please Rebecca. Rebecca insisted that they should eat together on this special day, and afterwards she went down to the beach for a final swim.

She lay for a while on the warm sand, wondering what she would do when she got back to London. She could not go back to work and she had spent most of her money coming here. The most sensible thing to do would be to remain here for a couple of weeks and return as though she had indeed taken a holiday, but she could not do that. She would not accept anything from Piers St. Clair, not his money or his pity.

It was very peaceful there on the sand. Somewhere along the shoreline she could hear the sound of music and guessed that a beach party was taking place at one of the other villas. No doubt there would be lots of people there, she thought, all drinking and talking and laughing and ... making love ... Tears pricked her eyes, but she would not give in to them. Self-pity helped no one, least of all herself, and she would not be such a fool again ...

The crackling of a twig behind her caused her to thrust herself up on her arms abruptly. It was dark behind her, the melting blackness of the swaying palms capable of concealing anything. She tried to convince herself that she had been mistaken, but it was no good, the feeling persisted, and even as she stared round with wide apprehensive eyes she saw a man emerge from the trees and walk down the beach towards her.

With an exclamation, she scrambled to her feet, but then she halted as the moonlight fell full on the man's face, illuminating the lean attractiveness of Piers St. Clair.

At once she was intensely conscious of the scarcity of her attire, and the tumbled silkiness of her hair. As before, he had her at a disadvantage.

'Hello, Rebecca,' he murmured, his dark eyes veiled and enigmatic. 'I am sorry it is so late, but I had some difficulty in obtaining a flight from Canberra.'

Rebecca stared at him disbelievingly, almost as though she expected him to disappear as unexpectedly as he had appeared. Then, she gathered herself and said: 'But it's Christmas Day! There are no flights on Christmas Day.'

'I know. I chartered a plane.' He glanced round abruptly. 'Do you suppose we could go up to the house? Rosa knows I have come down here and quite frankly she does not approve, for some reason. In fact I received quite a cool welcome from that lady.'

His words brought back to Rebecca all the contents of the letter which had arrived the previous day, and she realised why Rosa had behaved so strangely.

'I imagine Rosa was as shocked to see you as I am,' she said stiffly. 'Particularly as I don't recall inviting you. Or is it simply a case of you knowing that the villa is yours and I can't turn you away?' she finished fiercely, taking refuge in anger.

Piers stared at her for a long moment, and then he sighed. 'So you know,' he said expressionlessly.

Rebecca turned away to walk up to the villa. 'Yes, I know.' She managed to keep her voice calm. 'Excuse me, I must go and change——'

'Just a minute!'

Piers' hard fingers curved round the flesh of her upper arm, preventing her progress effortlessly. He brought her swinging round to face him and she saw that she had angered him. His expression was tense and unyielding from the way he looked at her she thought he wanted to wreak some terrible revenge upon her.

'I came here intending to follow a strict code of ethics,' he said harshly. 'I intended speaking with you formally in the light and civilised atmosphere of the villa with Rosa within calling distance, but when you speak to me like that you make me lose patience with you!'

Rebecca glared at him uncomprehendingly. 'Exactly

why have you come here?' she demanded, trying not to sound shaken. 'Has your—your bloodhound come up with some other terrible deed I've committed? Or have you changed your mind about giving me the villa? You needn't worry. I don't intend to stay here. I prefer my independence—I'm not a charitable institution!'

'Why do you do this?' he bit out angrily. 'Why do you speak to me thus? As though you hated me! Because I know you do not.'

Rebecca tried to wrench herself away from him. 'How do you know that?' she taunted him. 'Did Halliday tell you?'

'Rebecca, listen to me——'

'No! You listen—to me! I don't want your villa, your charity, anything to do with you, do you understand?'

Piers stared down into her upturned face for a long aching minute and then with a groan he shook his head and grasping the back of her neck he bent and put his mouth to hers, lips parted and demandingly passionate. Rebecca resisted for only a moment and then the pressure of his mouth and the seeking caressing strength of his hands destroyed all her defences, showing her more powerfully than words how hopeless it was for her to attempt to defy his mastery. The kiss went on for a long time and when he lifted his head it was but to seek the curving warmth of her shoulders and her breast. His fingers sought the securing fastener of the bikini top, but when she made no attempt to stop him his hands slid across her back and gripped her slender waist instead.

'You see!' he said, rather thickly, 'you don't hate me, Rebecca.'

Rebecca dragged herself away feeling humiliated by his demonstration of his power over her, but he caught her wrist, pulling her close to him again. 'If it's any consolation to you, I want you too,' he told her in slightly uneven tones. 'And that is why I am here.'

Rebecca's legs felt like jelly and she stared up at him appealingly. 'Piers, what do you want of me?' she whispered brokenly.

He regarded her troubled face with disturbingly penetrating eyes. 'Your face is so thin,' he observed huskily, tracing the line from the curve of her eye to her jawline with his fingers. 'You must believe me when I tell you I had no idea you had been so ill.'

Rebecca trembled against him. 'It—it was 'flu, that's all,' she said, trying to make light of it.

He shook his head. 'Paul told me. It was much more serious than that. But I was unable to come and see you for the simple reason that my arm was poisoned. You remember the accident, do you not?'

Rebecca looked at him closely. 'Of course I remember. You mean—the wound did not heal?'

Piers gave a faint smile. 'I would say that was an English understatement,' he remarked dryly. 'But it is of no importance now. There are other matters to discuss. The villa, for example.'

Rebecca swallowed hard and now when she drew away he let her go. 'Why did you do it?' she exclaimed. 'Why did you let me think this was mine when——' She bent her head.

Piers studied her intently. 'It is all yours. The lease was made over to you several weeks ago.'

Rebecca looked up quickly. 'But why? Why? Why let me think Adele had willed it to me?'

'It was the only way I could see to give it to you. I wanted you to have it. I wanted you to come here and get well again.'

Rebecca turned away. 'But you knew when I found out——'

Piers' eyes narrowed. 'You were not meant to find out. You never would have found out without someone's interference! As it is, you have already told me you will not accept it. What can I do? What can I say to convince you that I have no—what would you

180

say?—ulterior motives?' He smote his fist into his palm suddenly. 'Of course, this is not the way, I know that. Coming here, being angry with you, making love to you! This is not the way to convince you that my motives are altruistic.' He straightened his shoulders and indicated the lights of the villa. 'Come!' he said. 'You must not get cold. We will continue our conversation over a drink if you will be so kind as to offer me your hospitality.'

'How could I refuse?' Rebecca could not prevent the taunt which rose to her lips and she was surprised by the expression of pain that crossed his face.

'Please,' he said heavily. 'Let us go inside.'

Rebecca shrugged and without another word ran ahead of him across the grass and into the villa. On her way to her room she encountered Rosa. 'Monsieur St. Clair?' she exclaimed. 'Did you see him?'

Rebecca halted and nodded. 'Y—yes,' she replied almost reluctantly. 'He—he's coming in for a drink.'

Rosa frowned. 'I see. And you are still leaving tomorrow?'

Rebecca bent her head. 'Oh, yes, Rosa,' she said quietly. 'Yes, I think so.'

In her room she stripped off the bikini and as she had not bathed it was a simple matter to put on her underclothes and a simple white cotton shift that went well with her golden skin. She was thin, she thought inconsequently, and wondered if his reasons for observing this were an attempt to make her think twice before refusing the villa. She shook her head helplessly. With Piers St. Clair there could be no anticipation of his actions. He was unpredictable.

When she entered the lounge she found he was already there, standing by the window, not attempting to help himself from the comprehensive array of spirits that were contained in the cabinet. With an involuntary gesture she walked across to the cabinet and said:

'What will you drink?' in a tight, controlled little voice.

Piers lifted his shoulders. He looked particularly attractive, she thought, in a dark suit and a white shirt, his tan complementing his colouring, although now that they were in the light she could see lines of strain in his face which had not been there before and he too seemed thinner than she remembered. But then she recalled his poisoned arm and decided that was why he seemed to have changed.

'Do you have brandy?' he enquired now, and Rebecca looked down at the bottles.

'Of course,' she said, picking up a bottle of cognac. 'You should know...' Then she compressed her lips. She must stop behaving so shrewishly. Whatever his reasons for coming here she should not show him so blatantly how much he had hurt her.

She handed him his drink carefully, making certain that their hands did not touch, and he swallowed half of it at a gulp. Then he studied the remainder with critical intensity.

'To begin with,' he said quietly, 'I want you to know that Nurse Stephens was summarily dismissed from her post a week before Adele's death.'

Rebecca twisted her hands together, not attempting to pour herself a drink. She felt it would choke her. 'I see,' she said.

Piers looked up at her rather impatiently. 'Don't you want to know why?'

Rebecca pressed her lips together. 'If you want to tell me.'

Piers uttered an angry exclamation. 'For God's sake, Rebecca, try and be objective for a while. There's so much you have to know, and I'm finding it difficult enough as it is finding words to express what I have to say.' His dark eyes flickered over her. 'Believe me, I am not normally so forbearing.' Then he sighed. 'I'm sorry. As you can see, I am a poor apology for a counsellor, even when I speak for myself.'

Rebecca shook her head. 'Go on. I—I find it difficult, that's all, understanding why you are here. When
I was at *Sans-Souci*——'

'When you were at *Sans-Souci* I wanted to hurt you,
as you had hurt me,' he ground out violently. 'I did
not know then that it would be so many weeks before I
could see you again and explain.'

Rebecca stared at him. 'You mean—you didn't
mean what you said?'

Piers clenched his fists. 'Yes, I meant it. But not
quite as you seem to imagine,' he answered, finishing
his drink carelessly.

He came towards her almost compulsively, taking
her hands in his and sliding his fingers between hers.
He looked down into her face intently, his dark eyes
caressing, and she swayed towards him weakly. He
bent his head and kissed her eyes gently, and then
allowed his mouth to move caressingly across her cheek
to her ear, catching the lobe between his teeth. 'You
see,' he murmured huskily, 'I am not to be trusted
when you are around.' He kissed her mouth almost
hungrily, and then with determination put her away
from him. 'Not yet,' he said unevenly. 'I must go on.'

Rebecca moved away from him, and seeking a low
chair sank into it thankfully. For all she knew that he
found himself unable to keep his hands from her she
was still afraid. After all, everything he had said had
actually reinforced her opinion of why he was giving
her the villa and she ought to use her head instead of
allowing her emotions to run away with her. They
were alone here, apart from Rosa, and he must be
aware as well as she that he could seduce her defences
without any apparent effort on his part. She compressed her lips with intense self-loathing. Was she
such a fool that she would allow him to believe that
she was in any way different from the woman she had
always been?

Piers had poured himself another drink and was swallowing the raw spirit with obvious enjoyment. Then he turned and looked at her, leaning with negligent grace against the wall. 'Now,' he said, 'what was I saying? Oh, yes, Nurse Stephens.' He frowned. 'It was while I was ill and she was dressing my wound that I discovered she imagined she had some—how shall I put it?—interest in me.' He shook his head. 'I am not at all sure how she obtained this infatuation, but nevertheless, it was there, and I had to repulse it.' He looked at Rebecca broodingly. 'Does that sound arrogant? It was not meant to. But I have only ever loved one woman, and Sheila Stephens is not she.'

Rebecca coloured. 'I still don't see what that has to do with Adele.'

He fingered his glass experimentally. 'Do you not? No, perhaps I am not being lucid. It seems that Miss Stephens took the post for slightly different reasons than we had supposed. In any event, she chose to vent her frustration at this little setback on Adele, with the result that Adele became over-excited and I regret she had a rather severe attack. Of course , I dismissed Miss Stephens at once. Mrs. Gillean had heard them shouting and drew my attention to it.' He sighed. 'Unfortunately, although we obtained another nurse for my sister-in-law, the excitement was too much for her and a second attack proved fatal.' He swallowed some of his brandy, while Rebecca pressed a hand to her throat. She had not dreamed that Sheila had any other reason for writing to her than to try and wreck her happiness. It seemed she had personal reasons too.

Piers moved about the room rather restlessly. 'Naturally, I blamed myself,' he went on. 'After all, had I not been perhaps a little unkind to the girl she might never have behaved so carelessly. But a talk with Adele's physician convinced me that her condition had deteriorated since her return to England and there was nothing anyone could have done.'

Rebecca tucked her feet under her and then said: 'Why did she come back to England? Did you send for her?'

Piers regarded her sadly. 'Does that seem likely? Do I seem the kind of man who would invite such a woman into his house? No, of course I did not send for her. But she insisted on returning for Jennifer's funeral and she continued to stay on.' He lifted his shoulders and then let them fall. 'It was then that I began to realise how foolish I had been allowing her to come at all.'

Rebecca shook her head. 'She seemed to take a kind of vicarious delight in thwarting other people's attempts at happiness,' she murmured, almost to herself.

Piers looked at her. 'Your own, for instance,' he suggested.

Rebecca flushed. 'My affairs are unimportant.'

'Not to me!' Piers was abrupt. 'Never to me!'

Rebecca pushed back the heavy curtain of her hair. 'How can you say that when until I went to *Sans-Souci* you had forgotten my very existence!'

'That is not true!' Piers was angry now. 'Did I not ask you there about Halliday——'

'Oh, yes.' Rebecca's lip curled. 'Your investigator!'

With an exclamation, Piers went across to her and dragged her up out of her seat, holding her in front of him, his hands hard and cruelly biting on her shoulders. 'Very well,' he said huskily, 'it is obvious that you cannot accept my explanation without contradiction, so I must make it plain now that my motives for coming here are wholly—how would you say it?—honourable! I am not, as you seem to imagine, some kind of monster who imagines that because I cannot have you any other way I can offer a kind of bribe for your services! I have done many things in my life for which I feel shame, but where you are concerned I have no reason to feel so. Of course we have had our difficulties, of course when you left me to return to

England with your so-prim conventional morals disturbed I hated you! And why not? I loved you, I wanted you. I would have done anything in the world for you! The fact that I could not marry you was my only sin. And then it was a little sin, for Jennifer was never a wife to me!'

Rebecca turned her face aside. 'Oh, Piers!' she exclaimed.

'Oh, Piers, *nothing*!' He continued to hold her grimly. 'I want you to know how you hurt me then, because it was for this reason I did not follow you to England and force you to submit to me. And I could have done it, but you would have despised me afterwards, this I knew. So I buried myself in my work to the exclusion of everything else and for a time it was hopeless. Tom will tell you if you do not believe me. He knew something was wrong, but I could not tell even him, you had destroyed me so.' He closed his eyes for a moment and then went on: 'But I knew I had to know where you were, what you were doing, whether you were well. So I employed Halliday to discover your whereabouts and in his investigations he went to the hospital where Nurse Stephens still worked. It seems obvious now that she used him as well as he used her, for when Jennifer died and Adele came to England and advertised for a nurse, she immediately applied. Her references were good and after all, she was a good nurse. It was only afterwards I realised that she and Adele had become confidants and the story about Halliday was passed on.' He sighed. 'So many things happened, Rebecca; my wife was newly dead and it was impossible for me to seek you out then. Instead, when Paul wanted to take up the medical profession, I arranged that he should join the staff of St. Bartholomew's and in effect give me a reason for interesting myself in their affairs. You cannot imagine the horror I felt when I discovered that my son was—was involving himself with a young sister called Rebecca Lindsay!'

Rebecca put a hand to her forehead. 'So you knew all the time...'

'Of course. I knew everything about you. My intentions were that when a decent period had elapsed I would seek you out and offer you my life—such as it is. Unfortunately again, circumstances chose to prevent this and after Adele was dead I could think of no better way to help you and myself. The villa was mine. I bought it from Adele when it became obvious that she would not return to Fiji. I wanted you to have it. I could not let it be sold to a stranger, not after we had met there...'

'But you were sending me to Fiji, when you were in England!' Rebecca stared at him, quelling the impulse to believe that this was really happening—to her!

Piers sighed. 'Do you recall when you were at *Sans-Souci*, Tom was mentioning a job we intended to take up—in Australia?'

Rebecca's eyes grew clear. 'You mean—you mean—you were going to be in Australia?'

'I mean I wanted you here, near me, near enough for me to visit you and see you and show you that my intentions towards you were not to make you my mistress!'

Rebecca's cheeks burned. 'But——'

'But nothing. You were going to spend several weeks here growing strong again, and then I would approach you. Then yesterday, in Canberra, I got an urgent message from Tom in London. He had discovered quite by accident that Sheila Stephens had learned from Paul my intention to give you the villa. Knowing her as I have learned to, I guessed she might try to spoil things for you. Just as she tried to spoil things for me by telling me about your affair with Peter Feldman.'

Rebecca was horrified. 'But there was no affair...'

'I know that.' Piers smiled faintly. 'I regret to confess that I have a little knowledge of your sex and I am perfectly aware that you are completely unawakened when it comes to sexual experience——'

Rebecca would have drawn away then, embarrassed by his candour, but he drew her closer instead so that she could feel the hard strength of his body.

'So, you see, that is why I am here,' he murmured. 'I knew you would not allow yourself the luxury of accepting something of mine, and I had to see you and tell you...' He leant his forehead against hers, feeling the trembling awareness of her as she quivered in his arms.

'And now?' she whispered huskily, unable to think coherently any more, or wanting to.

'That is up to you,' he said quietly. 'I have put my—how do you say it?—cards on the table. Do you wish to take them up?'

'You said—you said Paul had spoken to Sheila. What—what does he know about—about us?'

Piers' eyes narrowed. 'Everything. I had to tell him. It was only right he should know.'

Rebecca shook her head helplessly. 'You once told me I could not love without security. Is that why you are offering me it now?'

Piers sighed. 'The only security is love itself,' he replied gently. 'Without it, there is nothing.'

Rebecca touched his cheek with tentative fingers. 'I was leaving tomorrow,' she said.

'Were you?' He watched her closely.

'I thought you felt sorry for me.'

'*Sorry?*' Piers touched her neck almost compulsively with his lips. 'I love you. I need you. And believe me, I have never loved anyone else. Oh, I admit I have made love to other women; I am no saint; I am a man with a man's failings and complexities, but with you I am young again, I am a boy with my head in the clouds.' He smiled gently. 'You are the only thing that matters in this crazy world of mine, and I want you in it always as my wife, able to share my name, my fortune and my bed...'

Rebecca slid her arms round his neck, loving the feeling of belonging that was enveloping her. 'Piers,' she murmured shakily, 'you know I love you. If you can forget all the things I've said I shan't ask anything of you. You have had one disastrous marriage, I should not ask you to risk another——'

But now Piers' face changed, and his eyes smouldered brilliantly. 'There is no risk with you,' he told her arrogantly. 'Without you I am only half a man, a shell of a being without heart or soul. Would you condemn me to living half a life simply because time got in our way?'

Rebecca shook her head helplessly. 'But Paul——'

'Paul will get used to the idea,' said Piers, his hands sliding over her waist to her hips. 'He is young. We have wasted so much time. Will you marry me? I am sure I can arrange it somehow, and afterwards we can be married again for all the world to see, but this will be for us. I simply cannot conceive of a long engagement...'

Rebecca pressed her face against his neck. So many thoughts flooded her mind, so many wonderful prospects had presented themselves. She thought with regret of Sheila and her abortive attempt to spoil everything. Rebecca felt she ought to thank her, for without her intervention it would have been several weeks more before paradise overtook her...

Poignant tales of love, conflict, romance and adventure

Harlequin Presents...

Elegant and sophisticated novels of
great romantic fiction . . .
12 all-time best-sellers.

Join the millions of avid Harlequin readers all over the world who delight in the magic of a really exciting novel.

From the library of Harlequin Presents all-time best-sellers—we are proud and pleased to make available the 12 selections listed here.

Combining all the essential elements you expect of great storytelling, and bringing together your very favorite authors—you'll thrill to these exciting tales of love, conflict, romance, sophistication and adventure. You become involved with characters who are interesting, vibrant, and alive. Their individual conflicts, struggles, needs, and desires grip you, the reader, until the final page.

Have you missed any of these *Harlequin Presents*...